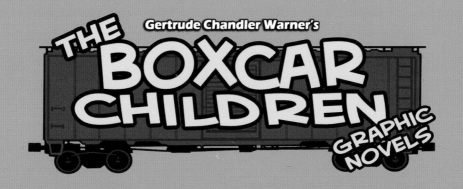

Gertrude Chandler Warner's

THE BOXCAR CHILDREN

GRAPHIC NOVELS

BOOK FOURTEEN
THE LIGHTHOUSE MYSTERY

When the Alden Children take a summer trip to the New England coast, they have a fun place to stay—a lighthouse! But strange things happen after it gets dark and Watch wakes up growling at night. Can the Boxcar Children shed light on a seaside mystery?

THE BOXCAR CHILDREN
GRAPHIC NOVELS

1. THE BOXCAR CHILDREN
2. SURPRISE ISLAND
3. THE YELLOW HOUSE MYSTERY
4. MYSTERY RANCH
5. MIKE'S MYSTERY
6. BLUE BAY MYSTERY
7. SNOWBOUND MYSTERY
8. TREE HOUSE MYSTERY
9. THE HAUNTED CABIN MYSTERY
10. THE AMUSEMENT PARK MYSTERY
11. THE PIZZA MYSTERY
12. THE CASTLE MYSTERY
13. THE WOODSHED MYSTERY
14. THE LIGHTHOUSE MYSTERY
15. MOUNTAIN TOP MYSTERY
16. HOUSEBOAT MYSTERY
17. BICYCLE MYSTERY
18. MYSTERY IN THE SAND

Gertrude Chandler Warner's

THE BOXCAR CHILDREN
THE LIGHTHOUSE MYSTERY

Adapted by Joeming Dunn
Illustrated by Ben Dunn

Henry Alden

Watch

Jessie Alden

Violet Alden

Benny Alden

magic
Wagon

visit us at www.abdopublishing.com

Published by Magic Wagon, a division of the ABDO Group, 8000 West 78th Street, Edina, Minnesota 55439. Copyright © 2011 by Abdo Consulting Group, Inc. International copyrights reserved in all countries. All rights reserved. No part of this book may be reproduced in any form without written permission from the publisher.

Graphic Planet™ is a trademark and logo of Magic Wagon.

This edition produced by arrangement with Albert Whitman & Company. THE BOXCAR CHILDREN is a registered trademark of Albert Whitman & Company. www.albertwhitman.com

Printed in the United States of America, North Mankato, Minnesota.
092010
012011
 This book contains at least 10% recycled materials.

Adapted by Joeming Dunn
Illustrated by Ben Dunn
Colored by Robby Bevard
Lettered by Joeming Dunn & Doug Dlin
Edited by Stephanie Hedlund
Interior layout and design by Kristen Fitzner Denton
Cover art by Ben Dunn
Book design and packaging by Shannon Eric Denton

Library of Congress Cataloging-in-Publication Data

Dunn, Joeming W.
  The lighthouse mystery / adapted by Joeming Dunn ; illustrated by Ben Dunn.
     p. cm. -- (Boxcar children graphic novels)
  At head of title: Gertrude Chandler Warner's The Boxcar children.
  "Graphic Planet"--Copyright p.
  ISBN 978-1-61641-122-0
  1. Graphic novels. [1. Graphic novels. 2. Mystery and detective stories. 3. Lighthouses--Fiction.
4. Brothers and sisters--Fiction. 5. Orphans--Fiction. 6. Warner, Gertrude Chandler, 1890-1979.
Lighthouse mystery--Adaptations.] I. Dunn, Ben, ill. II. Warner, Gertrude Chandler, 1890-1979.
Lighthouse mystery. III. Title.
  PZ7.7.D86Li 2010
  741.5'973--dc22
                                        2010016141

Gertrude Chandler Warner's

THE BOXCAR CHILDREN GRAPHIC NOVELS

BOOK FOURTEEN

THE LIGHTHOUSE MYSTERY

Contents

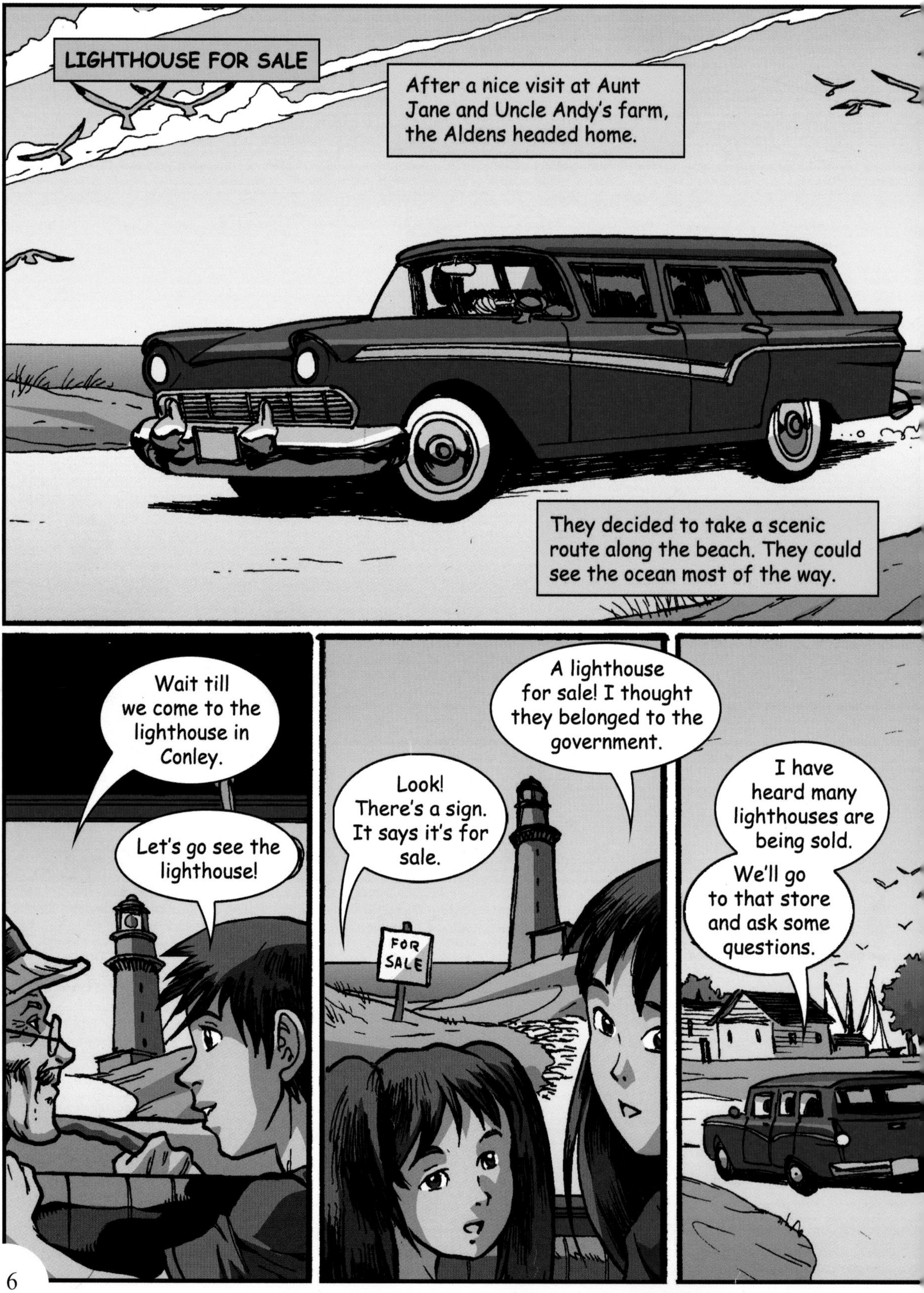
LIGHTHOUSE FOR SALE
After a nice visit at Aunt Jane and Uncle Andy's farm, the Aldens headed home.
They decided to take a scenic route along the beach. They could see the ocean most of the way.
Wait till we come to the lighthouse in Conley.
Let's go see the lighthouse!
A lighthouse for sale! I thought they belonged to the government.
Look! There's a sign. It says it's for sale.
FOR SALE
I have heard many lighthouses are being sold.
We'll go to that store and ask some questions.

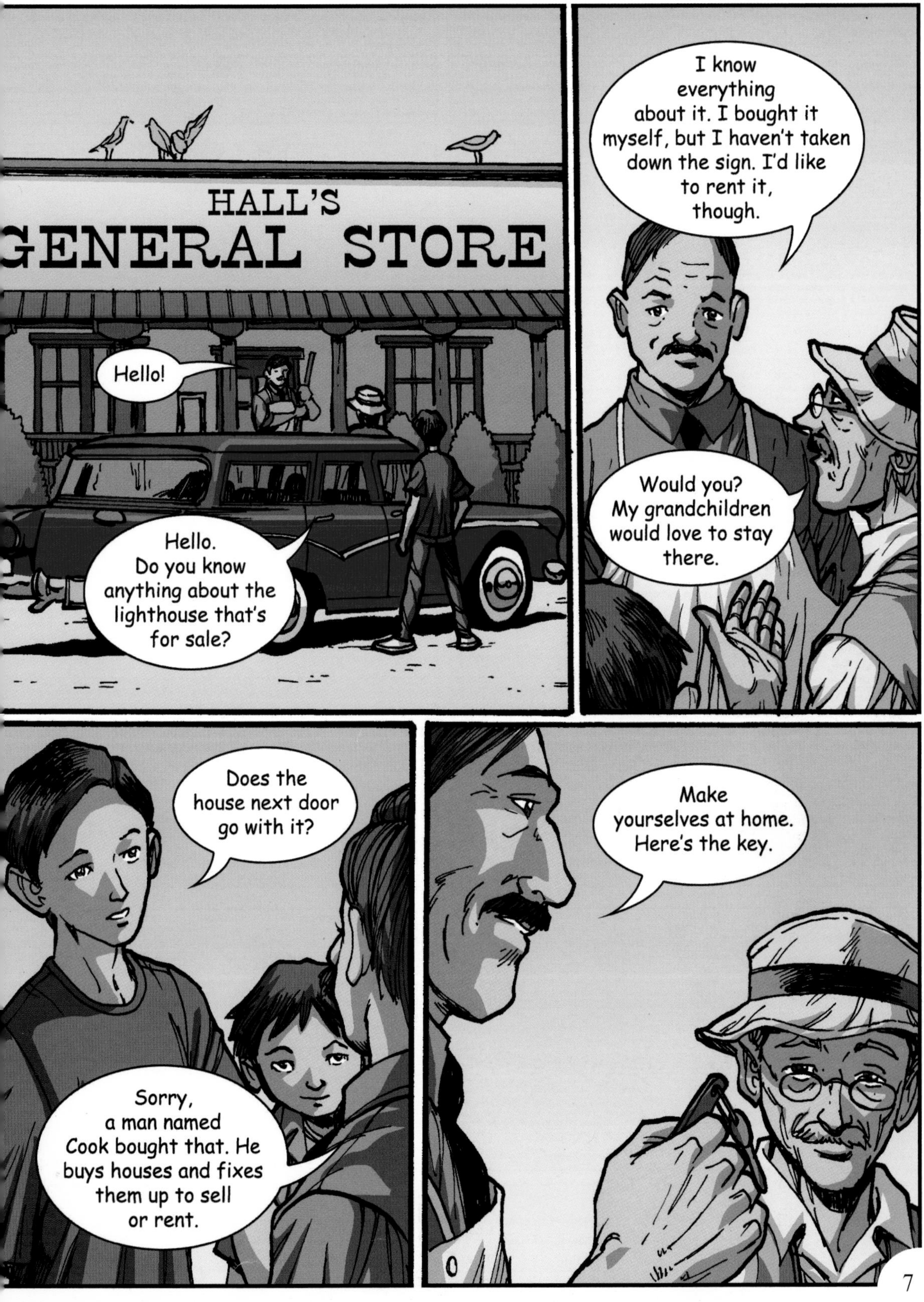
HALL'S
GENERAL STORE
Hello!
Hello. Do you know anything about the lighthouse that's for sale?
I know everything about it. I bought it myself, but I haven't taken down the sign. I'd like to rent it, though.
Would you? My grandchildren would love to stay there.
Does the house next door go with it?
Sorry, a man named Cook bought that. He buys houses and fixes them up to sell or rent.
Make yourselves at home. Here's the key.

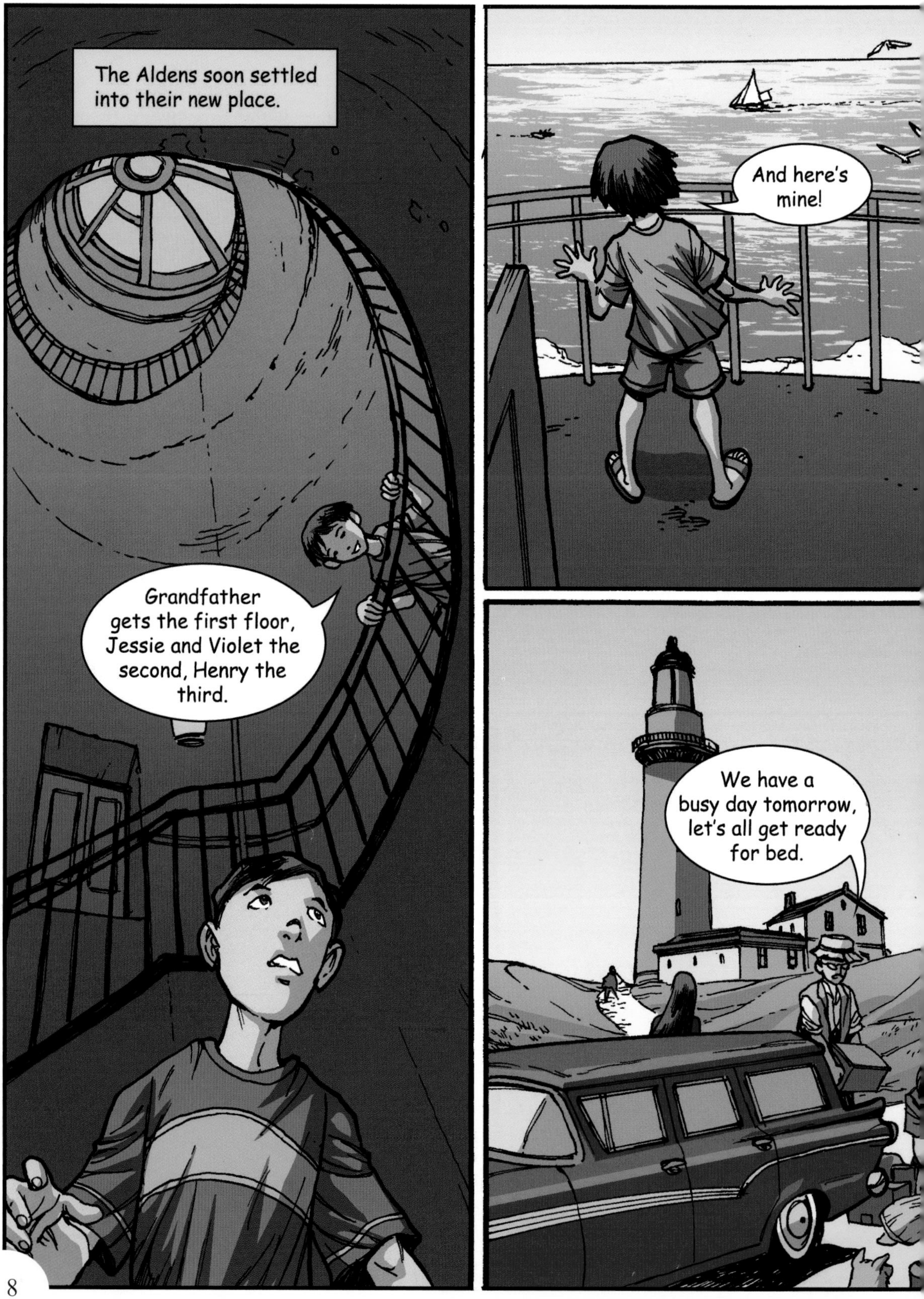
The Aldens soon settled into their new place.
Grandfather gets the first floor, Jessie and Violet the second, Henry the third.
And here's mine!
We have a busy day tomorrow, let's all get ready for bed.

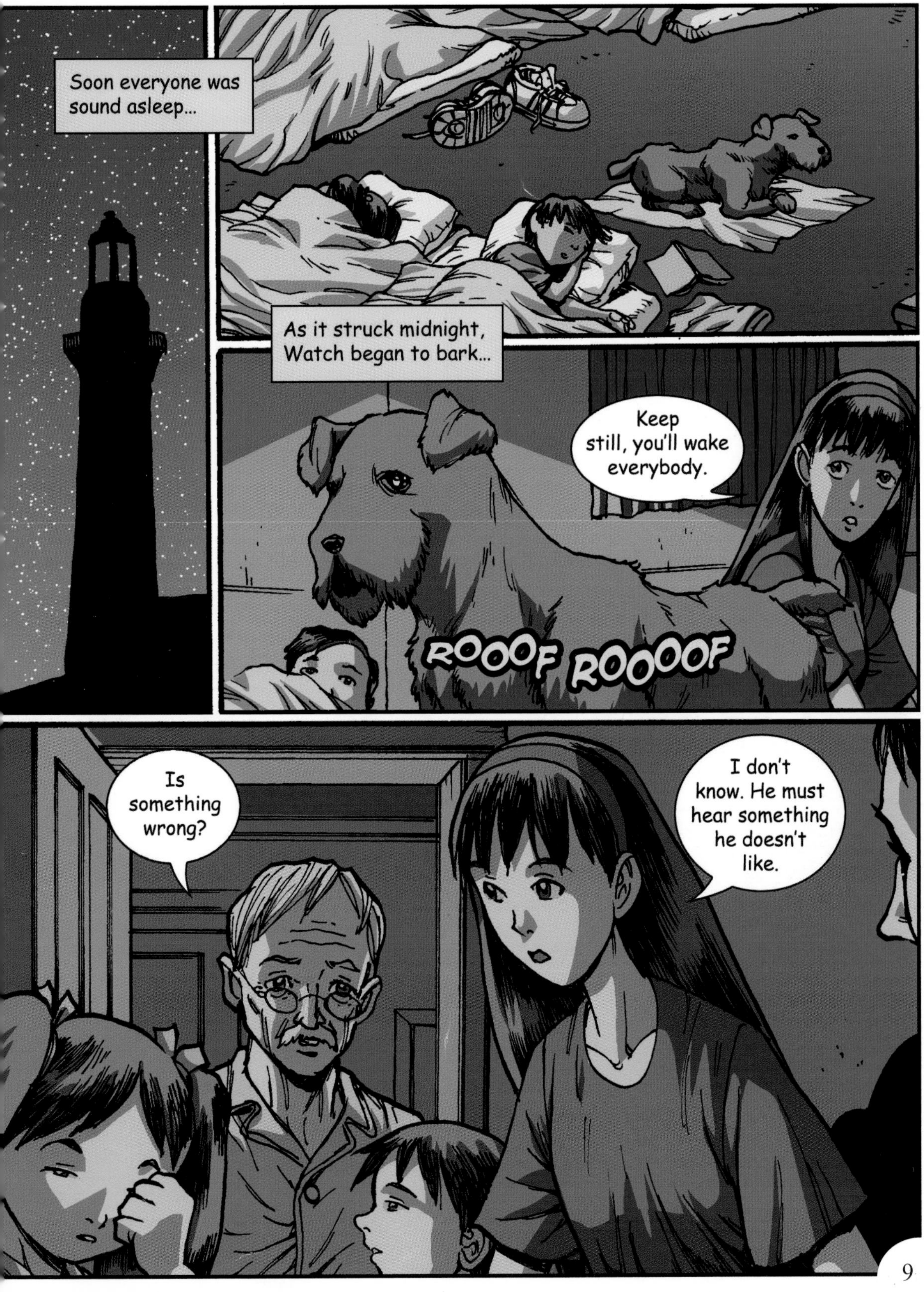
Soon everyone was sound asleep...
As it struck midnight, Watch began to bark...
Keep still, you'll wake everybody.
ROOOF ROOOOF
Is something wrong?
I don't know. He must hear something he doesn't like.

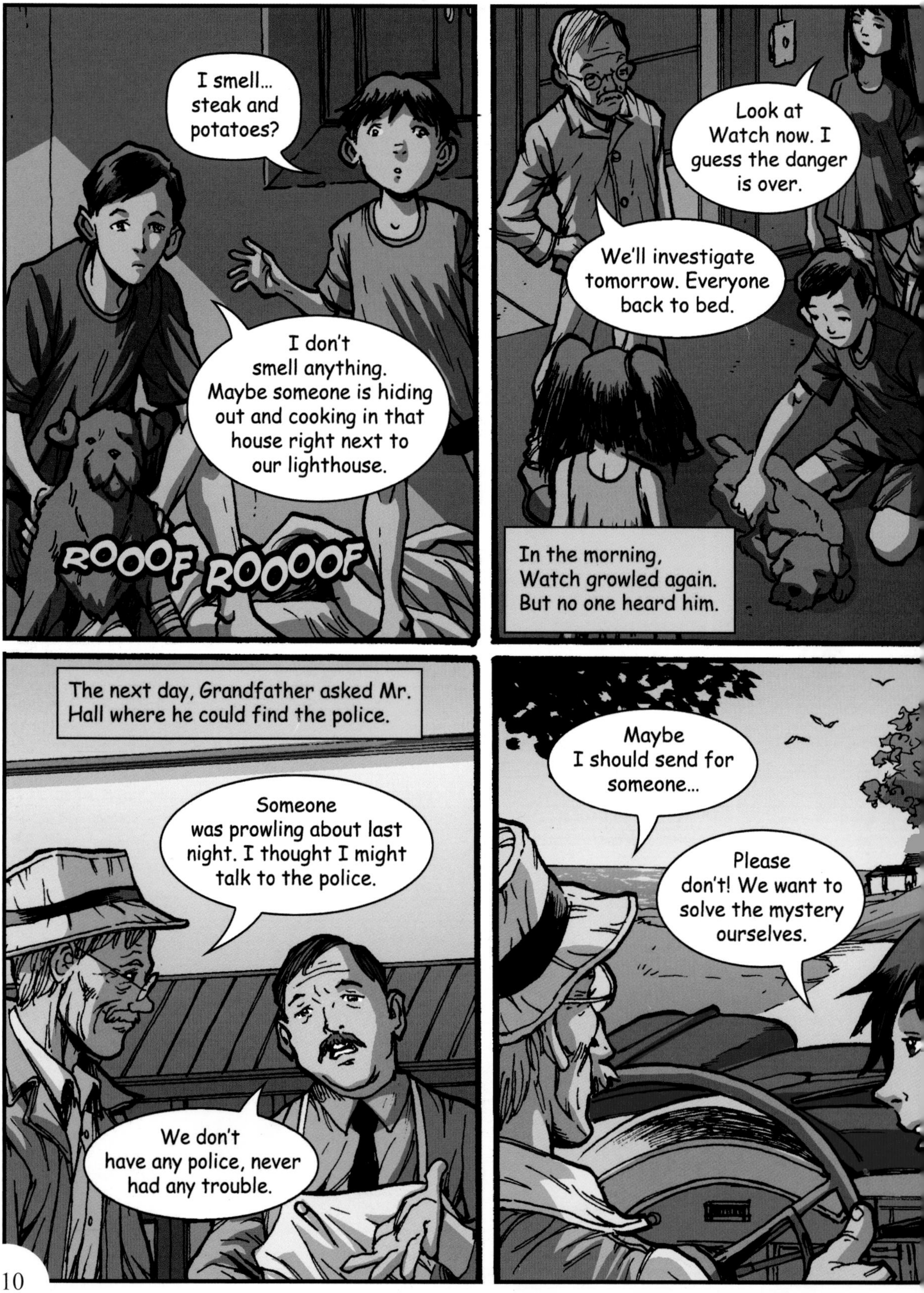
I smell... steak and potatoes?
I don't smell anything. Maybe someone is hiding out and cooking in that house right next to our lighthouse.
ROOOF ROOOOF
Look at Watch now. I guess the danger is over.
We'll investigate tomorrow. Everyone back to bed.
In the morning, Watch growled again. But no one heard him.
The next day, Grandfather asked Mr. Hall where he could find the police.
Someone was prowling about last night. I thought I might talk to the police.
We don't have any police, never had any trouble.
Maybe I should send for someone...
Please don't! We want to solve the mystery ourselves.

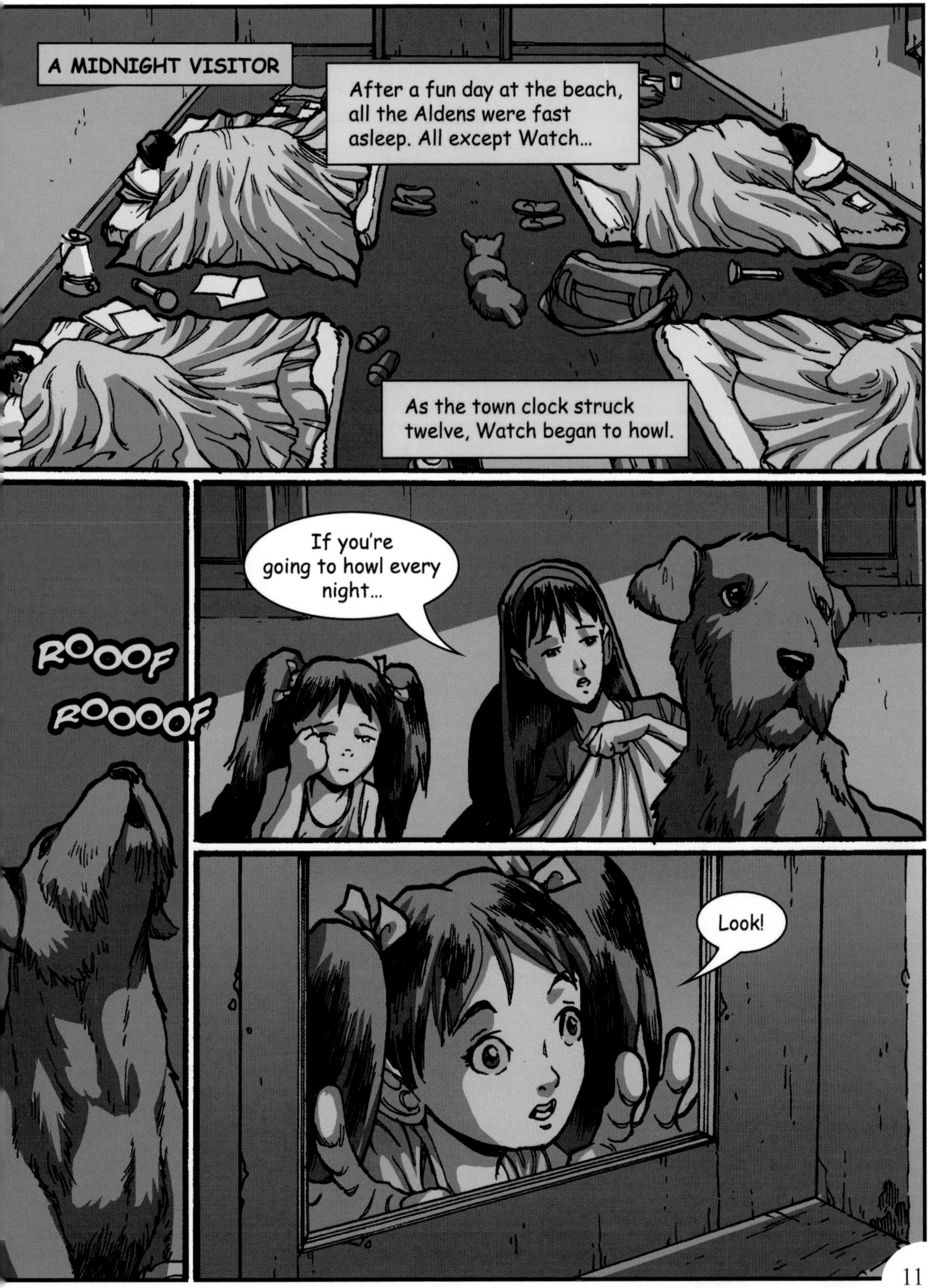
A MIDNIGHT VISITOR
After a fun day at the beach, all the Aldens were fast asleep. All except Watch...
As the town clock struck twelve, Watch began to howl.
ROOOF
ROOOOF
If you're going to howl every night...
Look!

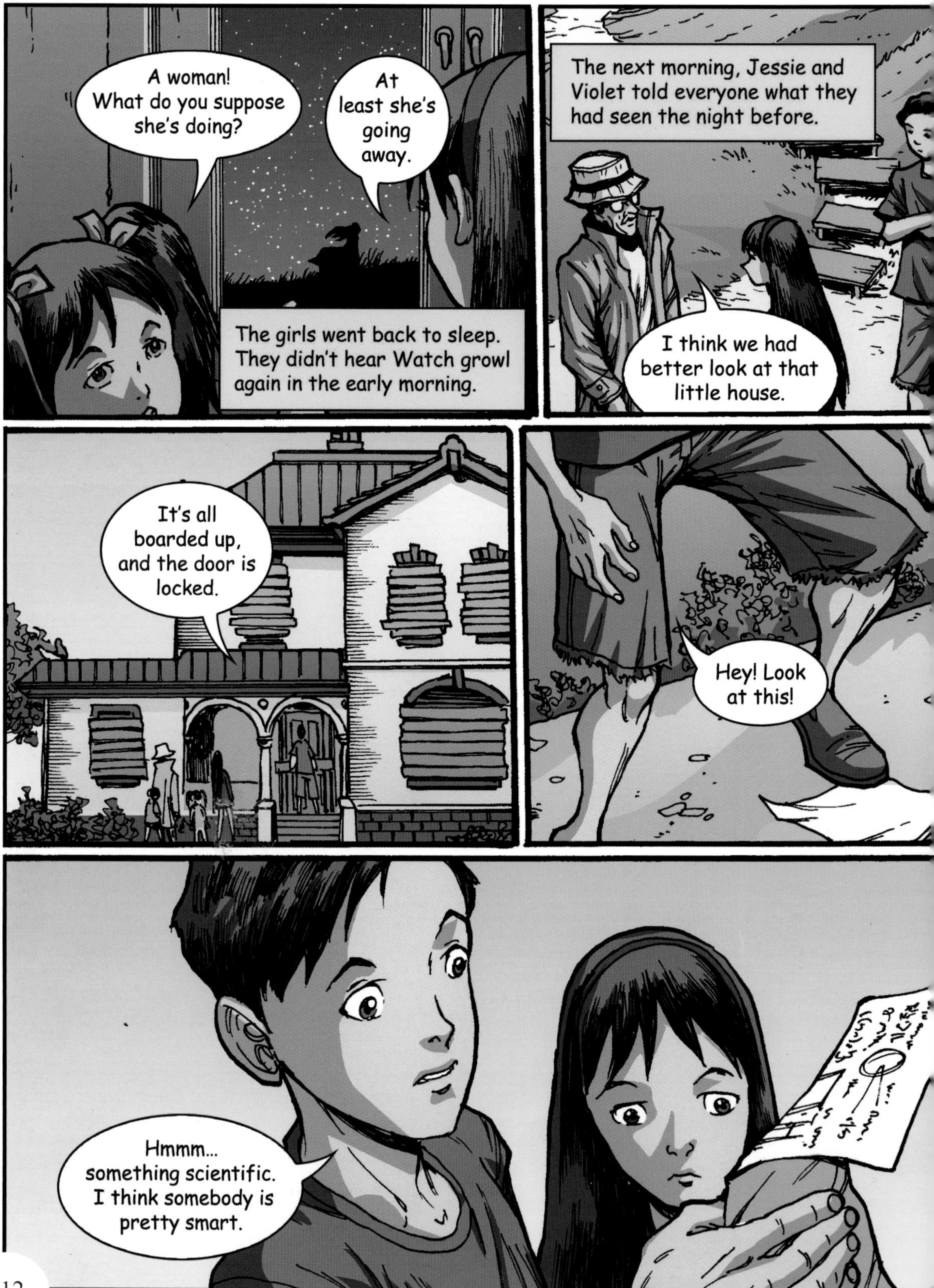
A woman!
What do you suppose she's doing?
At least she's going away.
The girls went back to sleep. They didn't hear Watch growl again in the early morning.
The next morning, Jessie and Violet told everyone what they had seen the night before.
I think we had better look at that little house.
It's all boarded up, and the door is locked.
Hey! Look at this!
Hmmm... something scientific. I think somebody is pretty smart.

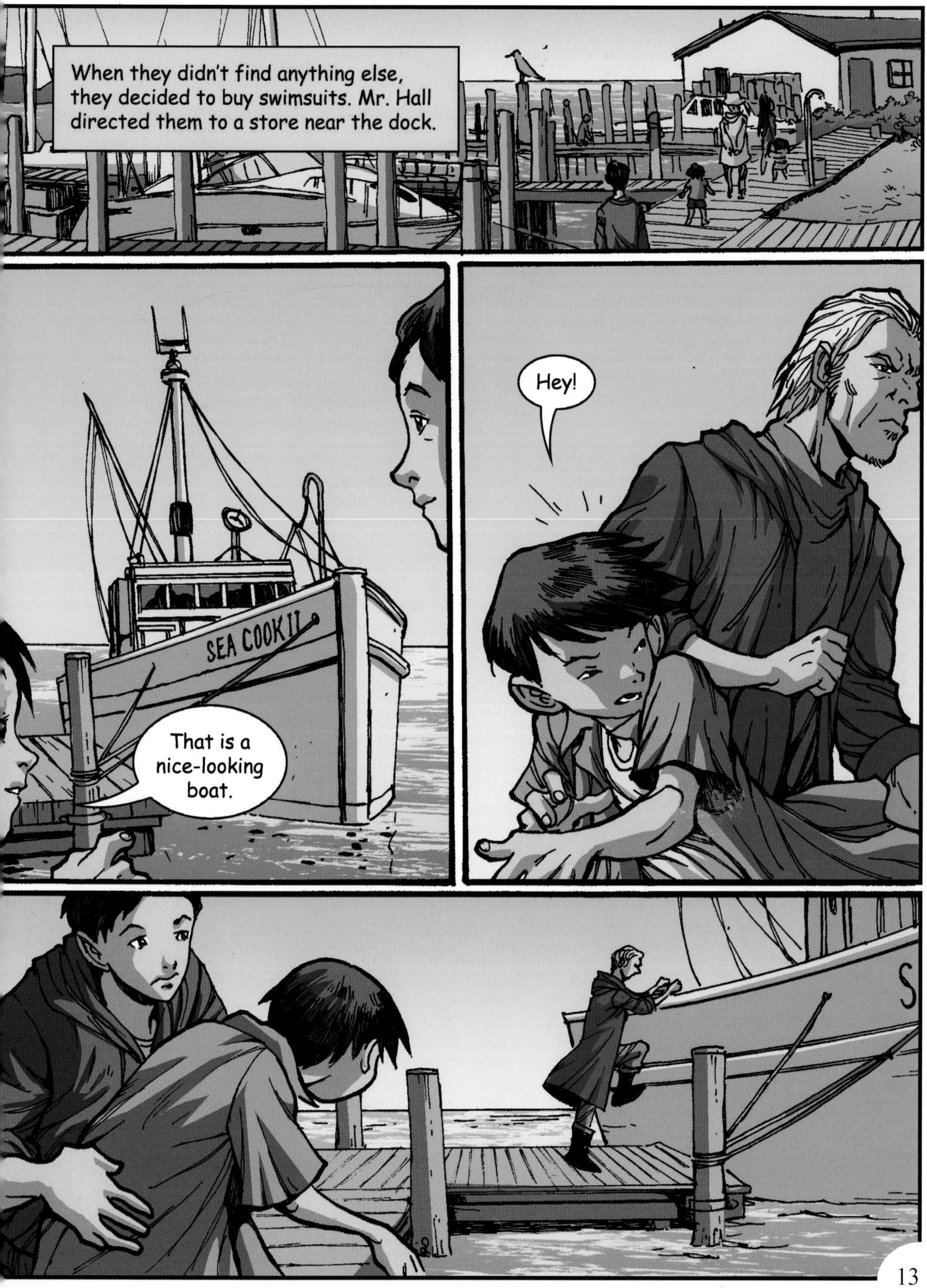
When they didn't find anything else, they decided to buy swimsuits. Mr. Hall directed them to a store near the dock.
SEA COOK II
That is a nice-looking boat.
Hey!

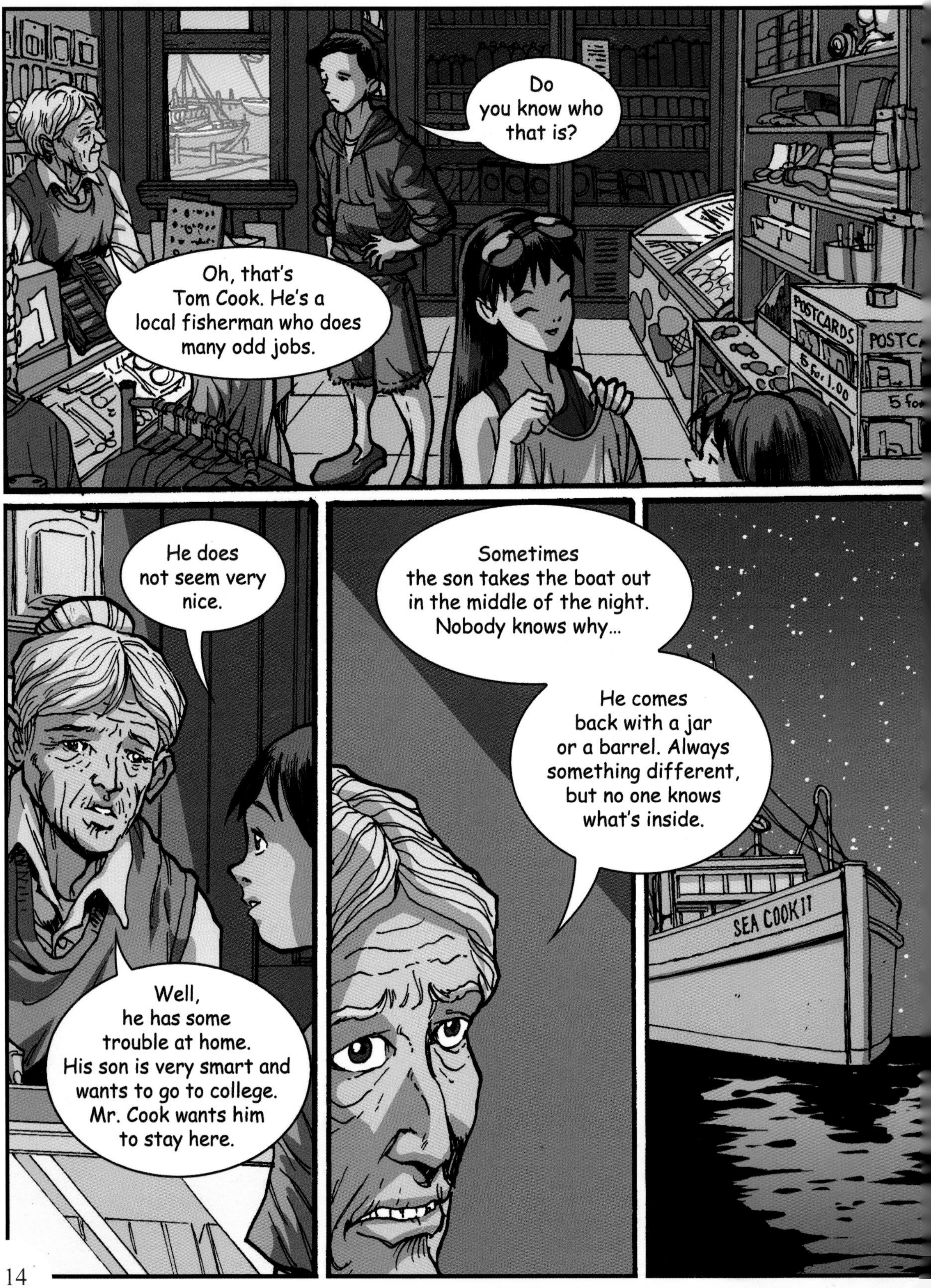
Do you know who that is?
Oh, that's Tom Cook. He's a local fisherman who does many odd jobs.
POSTCARDS
5 for 1.00
POSTC
5 for
He does not seem very nice.
Well, he has some trouble at home. His son is very smart and wants to go to college. Mr. Cook wants him to stay here.
Sometimes the son takes the boat out in the middle of the night. Nobody knows why...
He comes back with a jar or a barrel. Always something different, but no one knows what's inside.
SEA COOK II

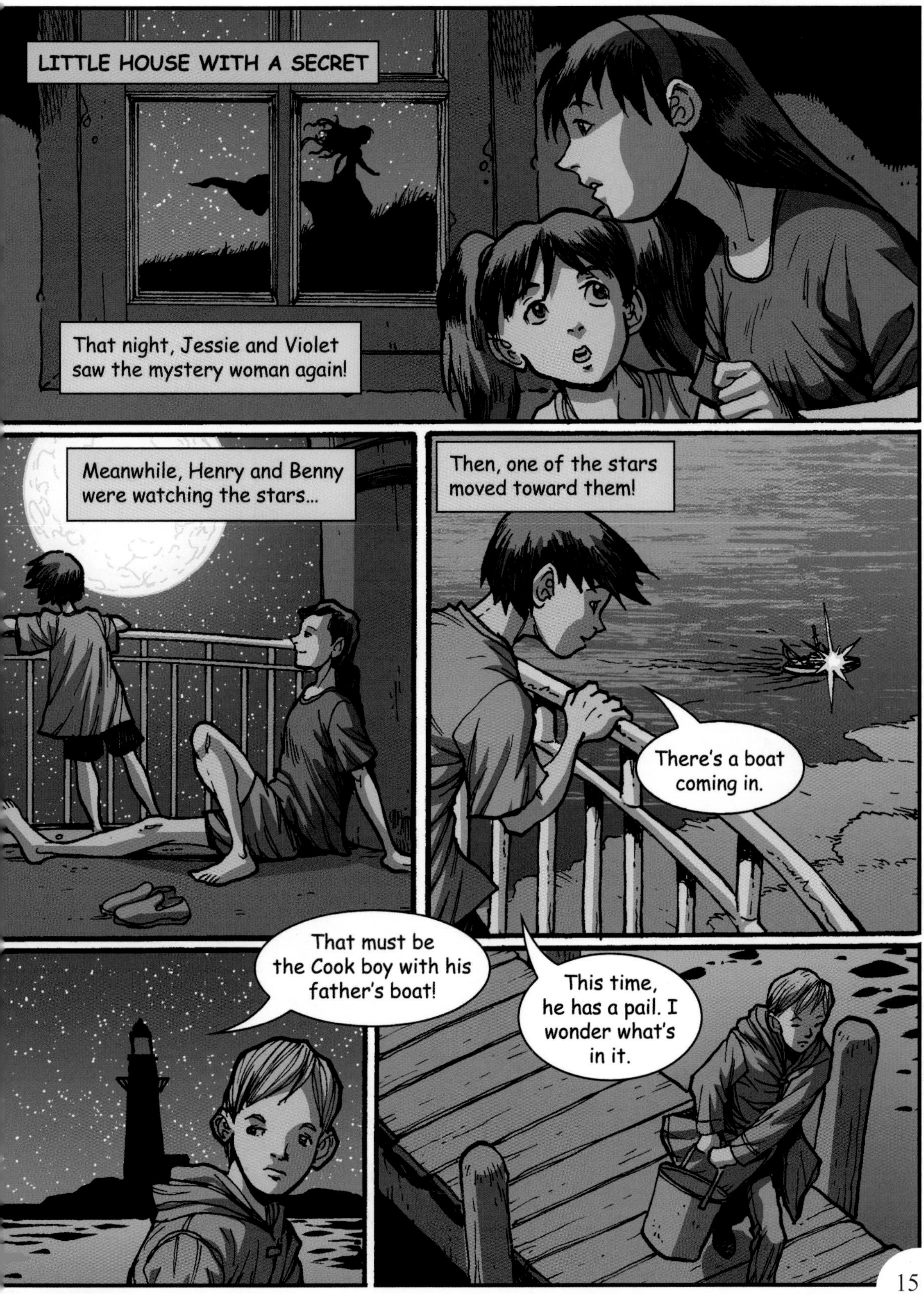
LITTLE HOUSE WITH A SECRET
That night, Jessie and Violet saw the mystery woman again!
Meanwhile, Henry and Benny were watching the stars...
Then, one of the stars moved toward them!
There's a boat coming in.
That must be the Cook boy with his father's boat!
This time, he has a pail. I wonder what's in it.

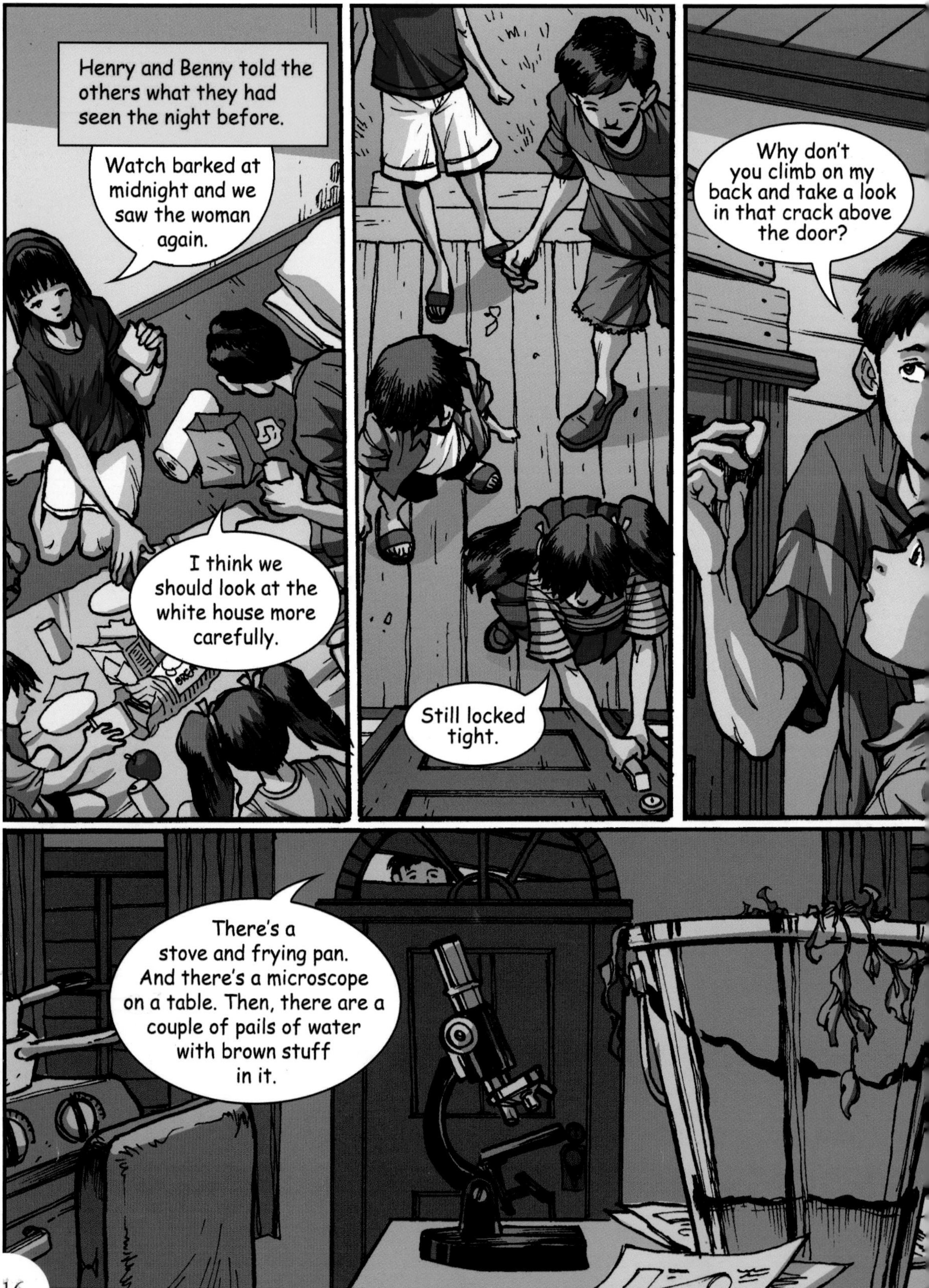
Henry and Benny told the others what they had seen the night before.
Watch barked at midnight and we saw the woman again.
I think we should look at the white house more carefully.
Still locked tight.
Why don't you climb on my back and take a look in that crack above the door?
There's a stove and frying pan. And there's a microscope on a table. Then, there are a couple of pails of water with brown stuff in it.

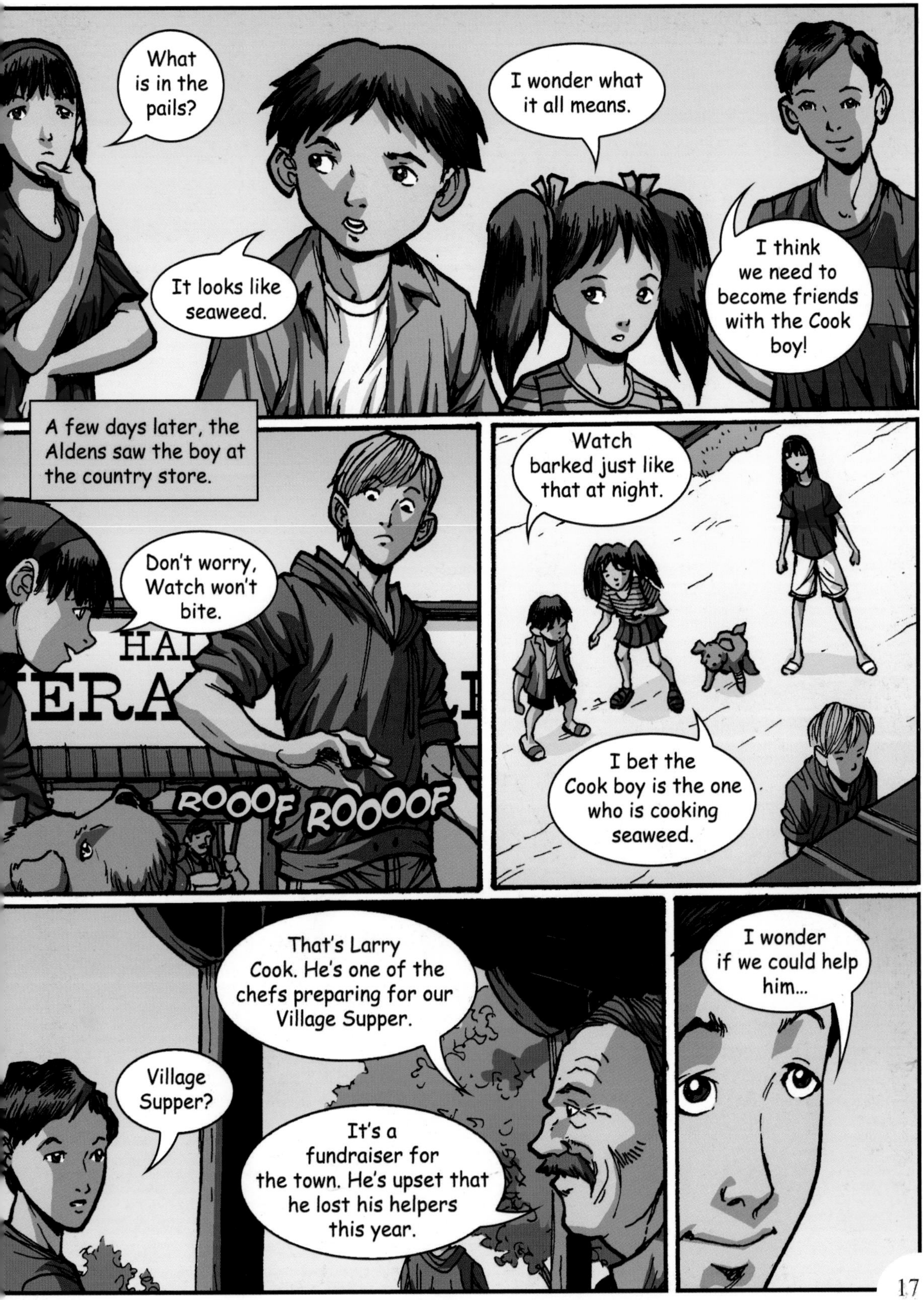
What is in the pails?
I wonder what it all means.
It looks like seaweed.
I think we need to become friends with the Cook boy!
A few days later, the Aldens saw the boy at the country store.
Don't worry, Watch won't bite.
ROOOF ROOOOF
Watch barked just like that at night.
I bet the Cook boy is the one who is cooking seaweed.
That's Larry Cook. He's one of the chefs preparing for our Village Supper.
Village Supper?
It's a fundraiser for the town. He's upset that he lost his helpers this year.
I wonder if we could help him...

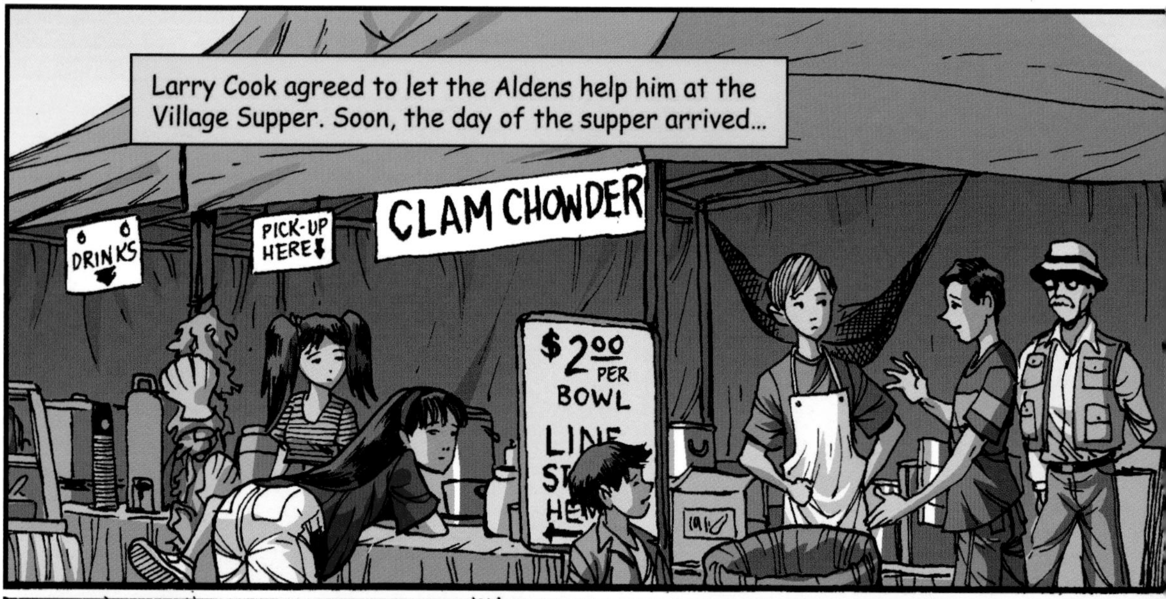
Larry Cook agreed to let the Aldens help him at the Village Supper. Soon, the day of the supper arrived...
CLAM CHOWDER
DRINKS
PICK-UP HERE
$2.00 PER BOWL

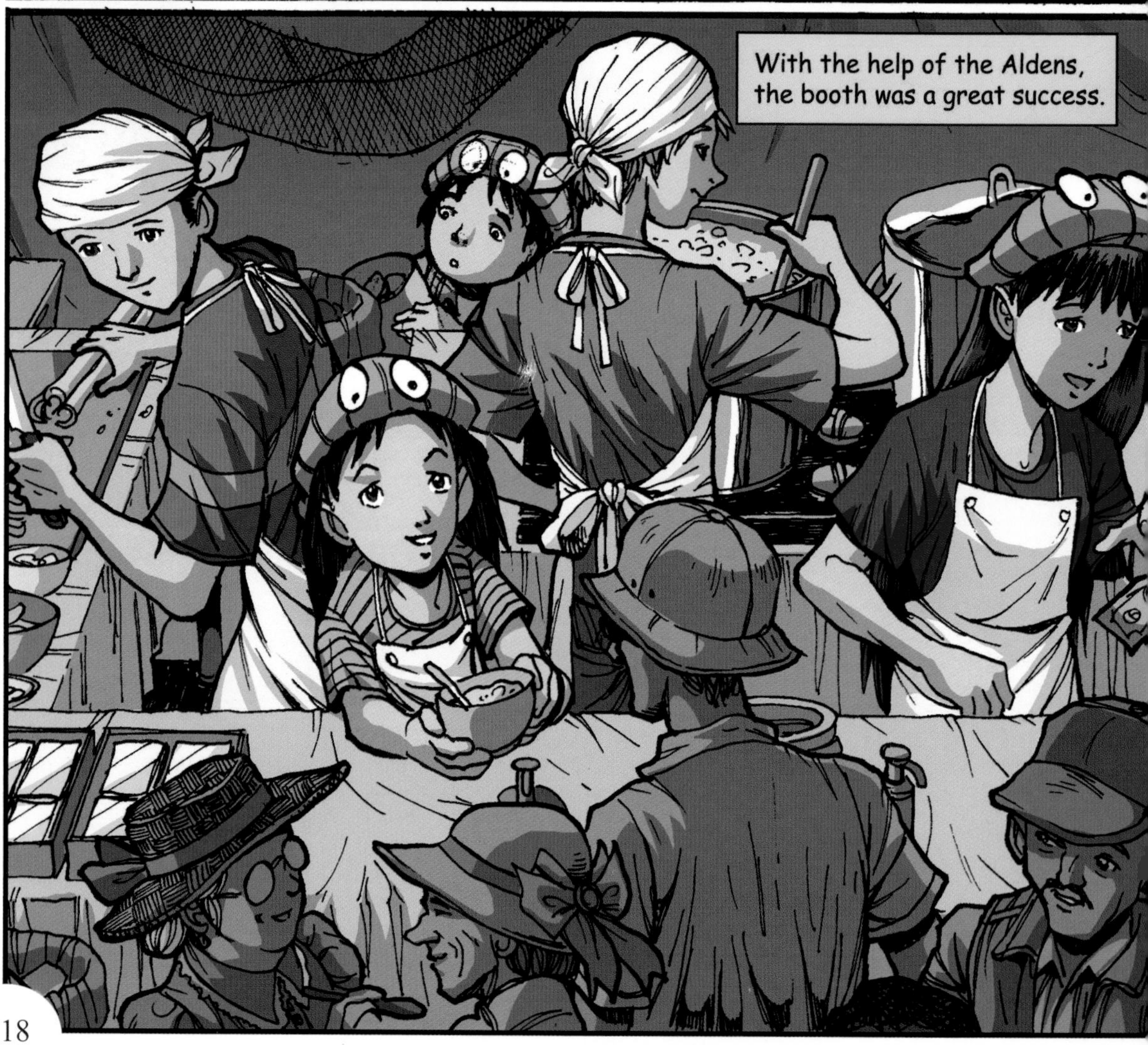
With the help of the Aldens, the booth was a great success.

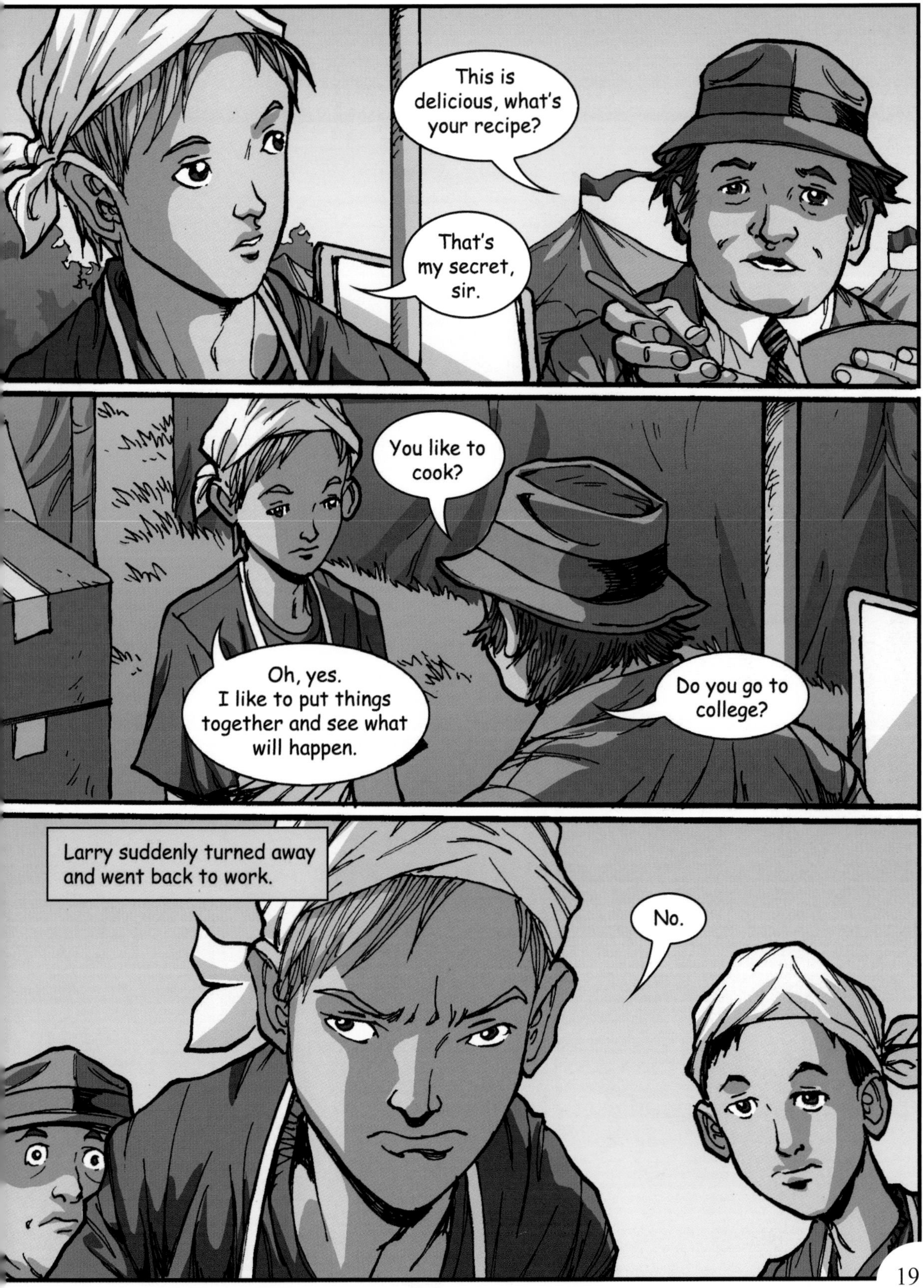
This is delicious, what's your recipe?
That's my secret, sir.
You like to cook?
Oh, yes. I like to put things together and see what will happen.
Do you go to college?
Larry suddenly turned away and went back to work.
No.

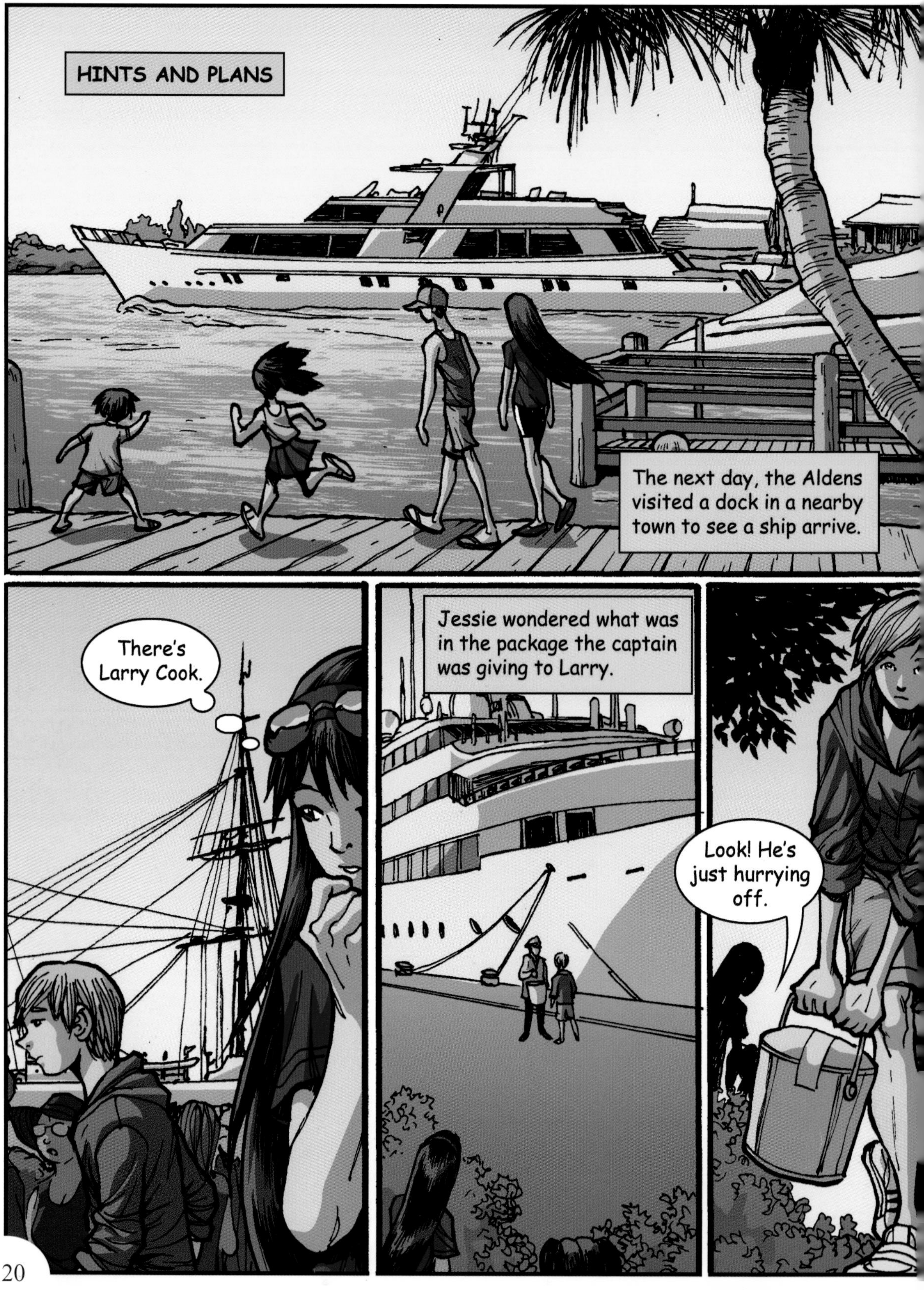
HINTS AND PLANS
The next day, the Aldens visited a dock in a nearby town to see a ship arrive.
There's Larry Cook.
Jessie wondered what was in the package the captain was giving to Larry.
Look! He's just hurrying off.

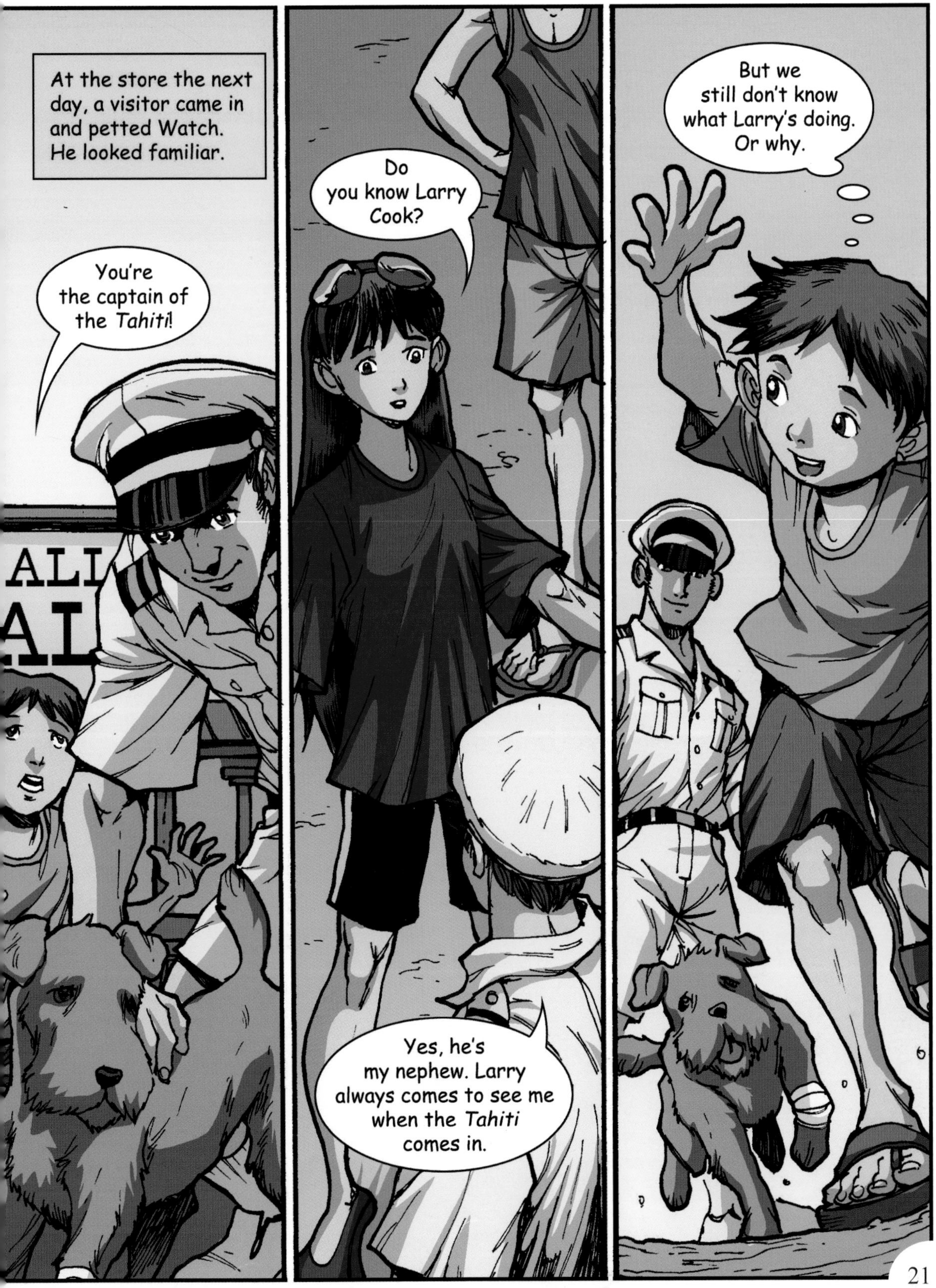
At the store the next day, a visitor came in and petted Watch. He looked familiar.
You're the captain of the *Tahiti*!
Do you know Larry Cook?
Yes, he's my nephew. Larry always comes to see me when the *Tahiti* comes in.
But we still don't know what Larry's doing. Or why.

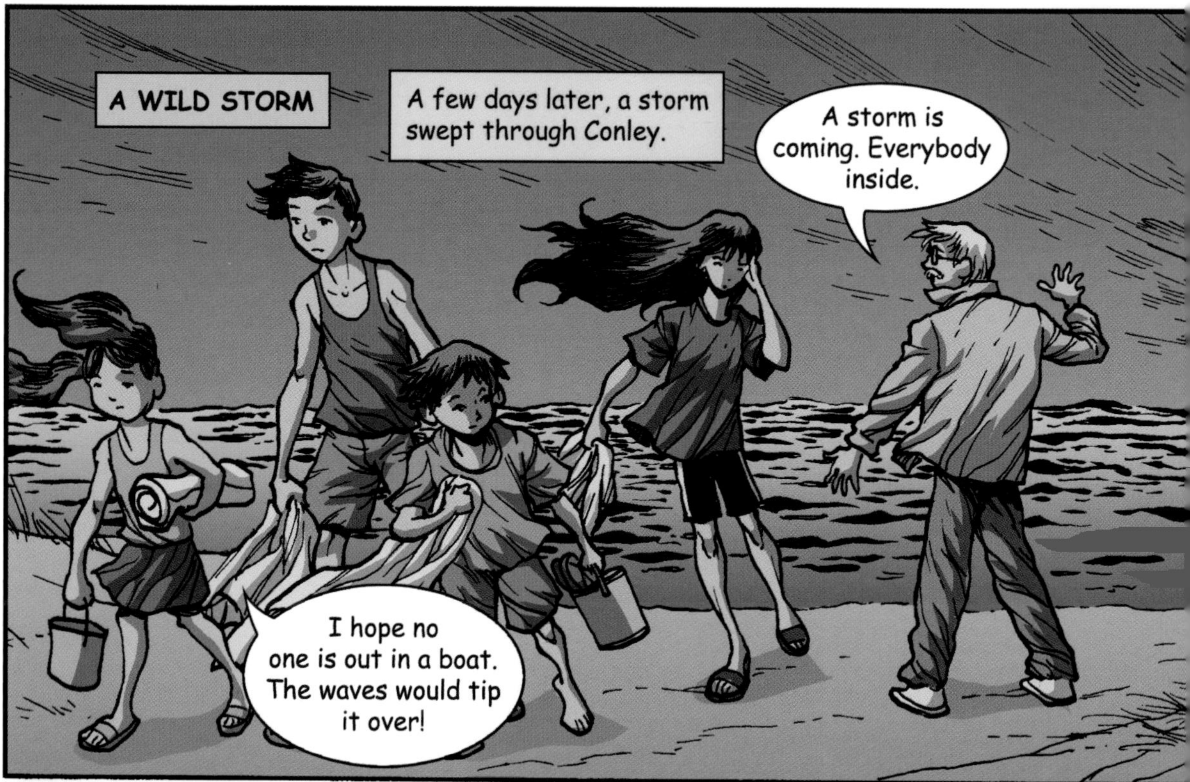
A WILD STORM
A few days later, a storm swept through Conley.
A storm is coming. Everybody inside.
I hope no one is out in a boat. The waves would tip it over!

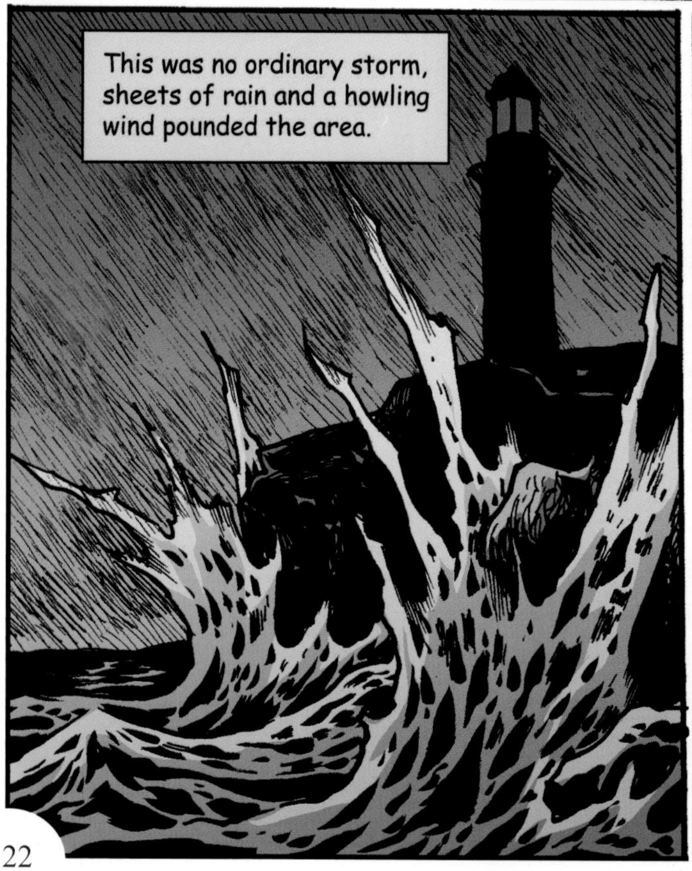
This was no ordinary storm, sheets of rain and a howling wind pounded the area.

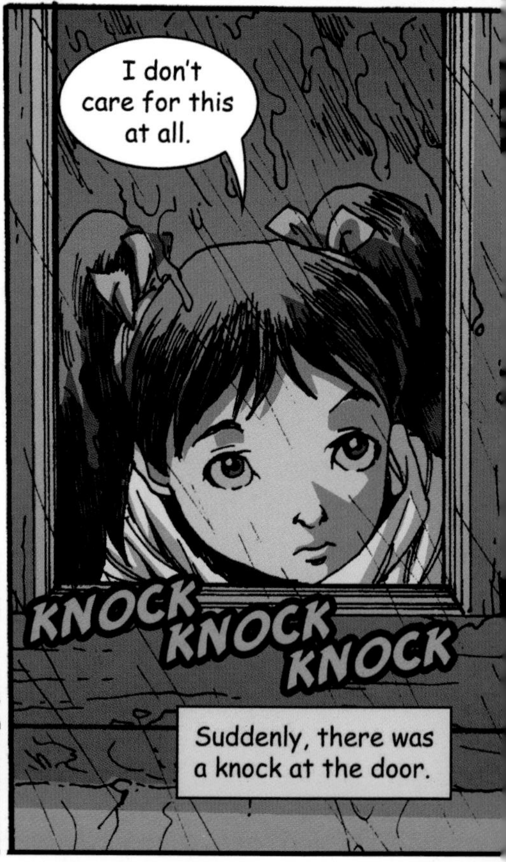
I don't care for this at all.
KNOCK KNOCK KNOCK
Suddenly, there was a knock at the door.

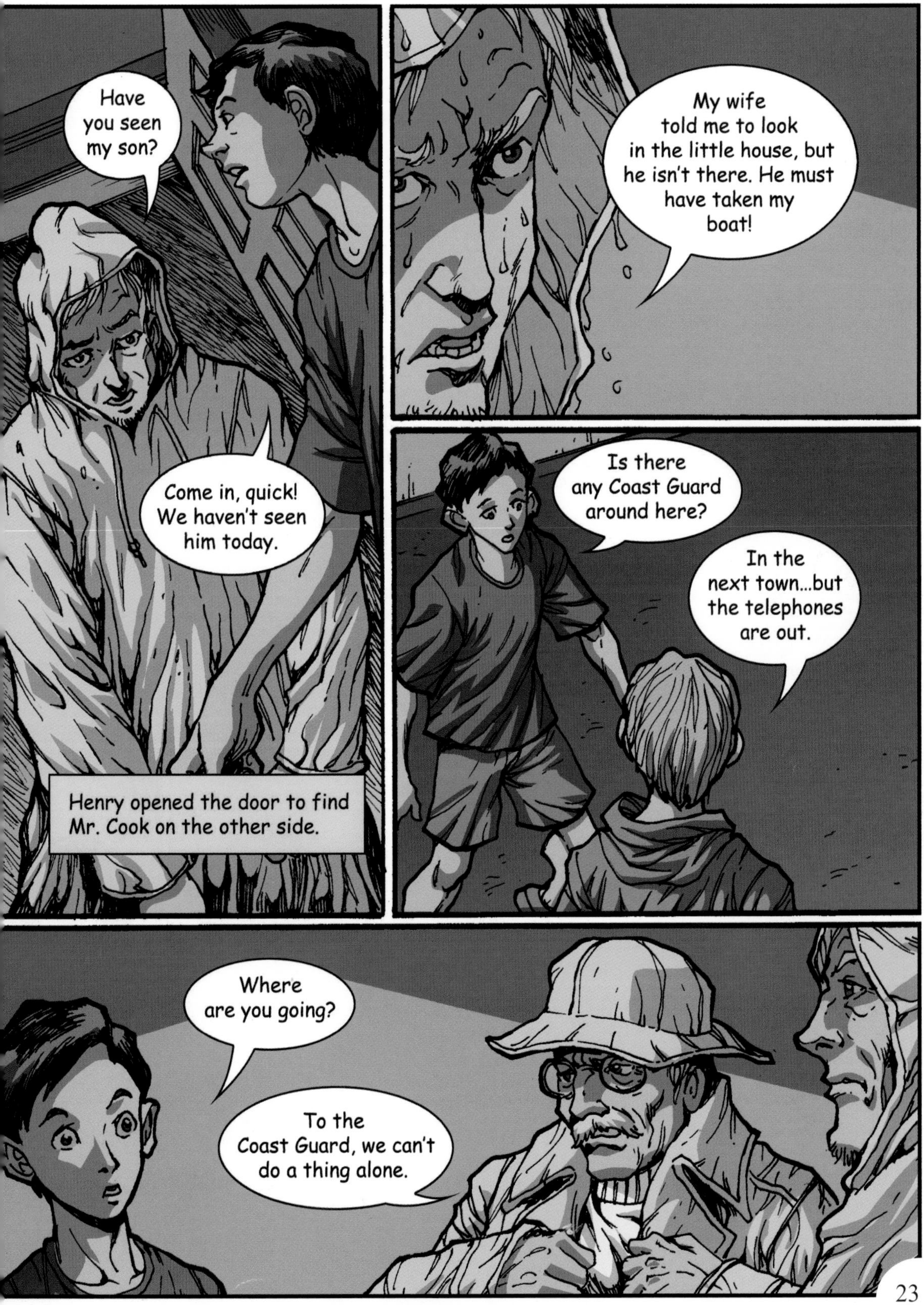

Have you seen my son?
Come in, quick! We haven't seen him today.
Henry opened the door to find Mr. Cook on the other side.
My wife told me to look in the little house, but he isn't there. He must have taken my boat!
Is there any Coast Guard around here?
In the next town...but the telephones are out.
Where are you going?
To the Coast Guard, we can't do a thing alone.

Grandfather and Mr. Cook were quickly on their way.

Grandfather will make it. He always does.

I'm going to try to help.

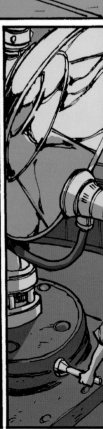

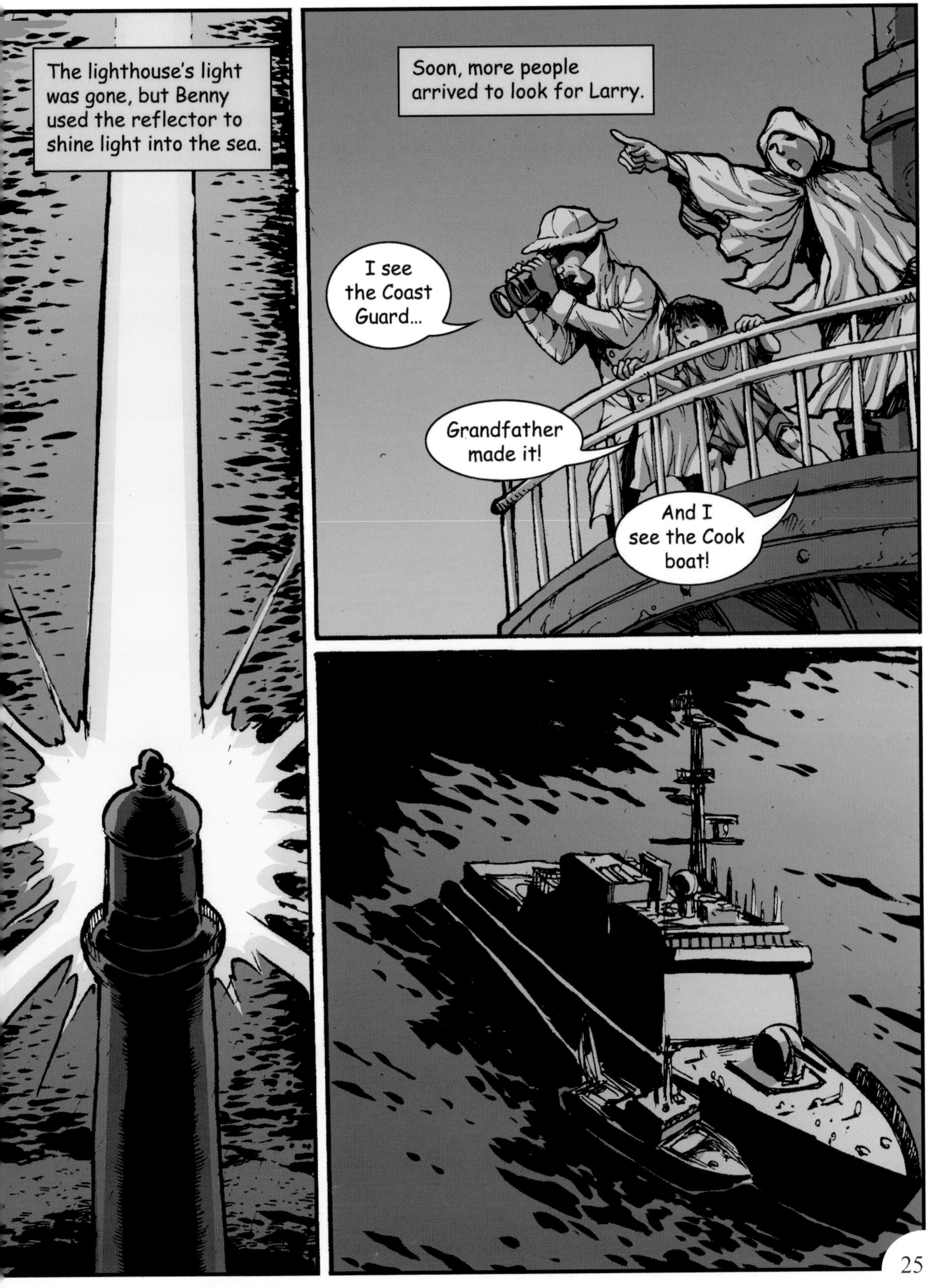
The lighthouse's light was gone, but Benny used the reflector to shine light into the sea.
Soon, more people arrived to look for Larry.
I see the Coast Guard...
Grandfather made it!
And I see the Cook boat!

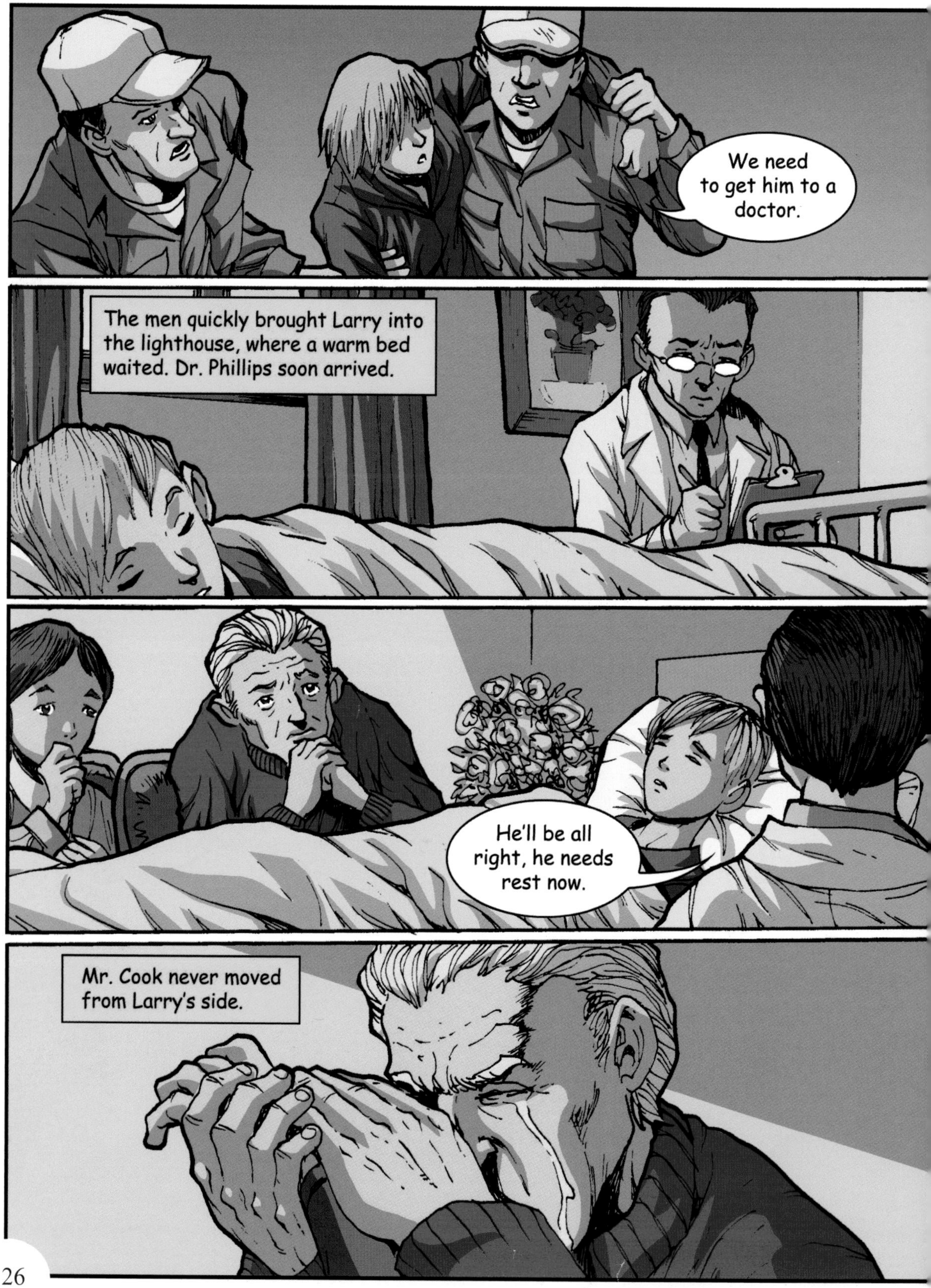
We need to get him to a doctor.
The men quickly brought Larry into the lighthouse, where a warm bed waited. Dr. Phillips soon arrived.
He'll be all right, he needs rest now.
Mr. Cook never moved from Larry's side.

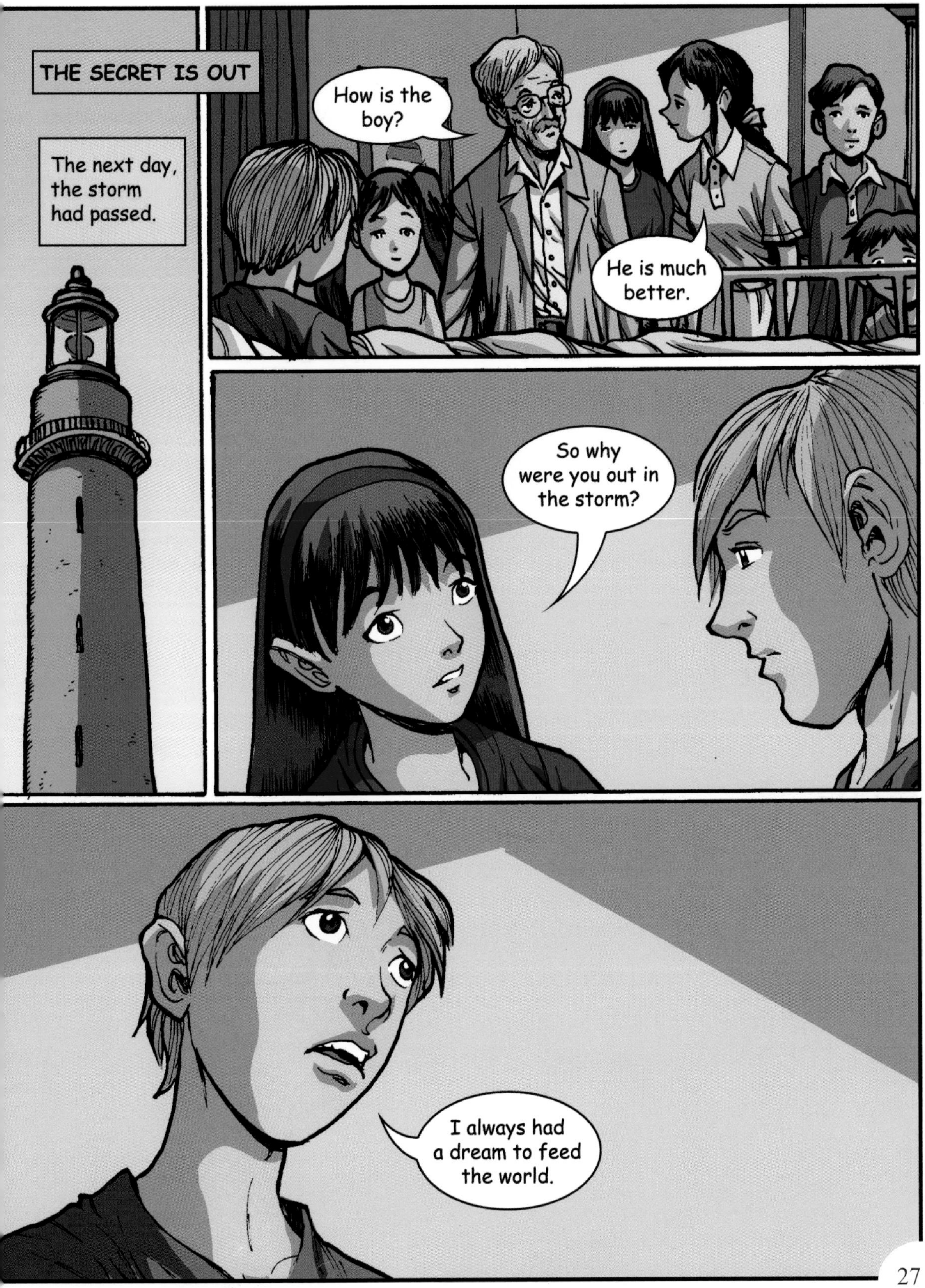
THE SECRET IS OUT
The next day, the storm had passed.
How is the boy?
He is much better.
So why were you out in the storm?
I always had a dream to feed the world.

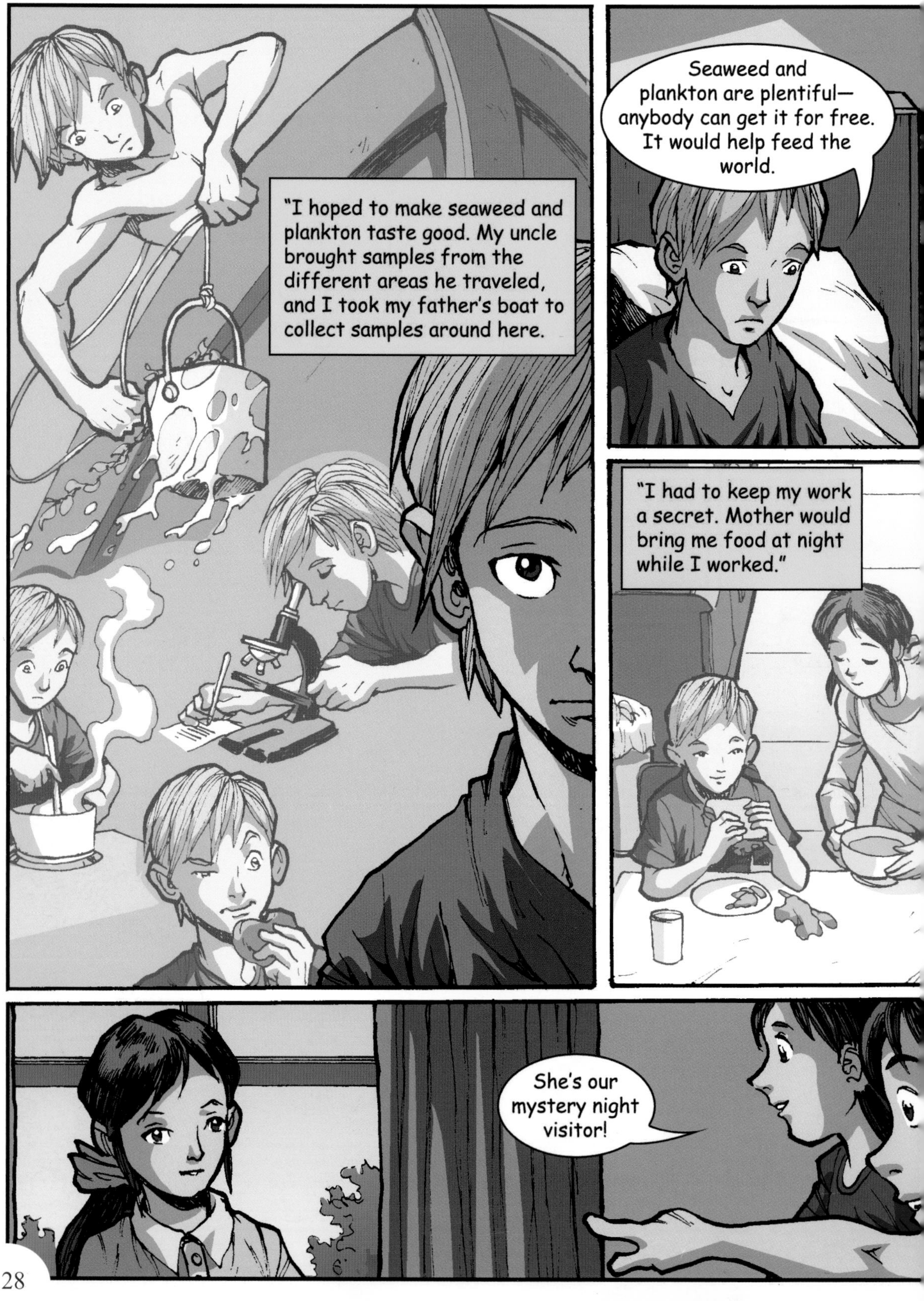
"I hoped to make seaweed and plankton taste good. My uncle brought samples from the different areas he traveled, and I took my father's boat to collect samples around here.
Seaweed and plankton are plentiful—anybody can get it for free. It would help feed the world.
"I had to keep my work a secret. Mother would bring me food at night while I worked."
She's our mystery night visitor!

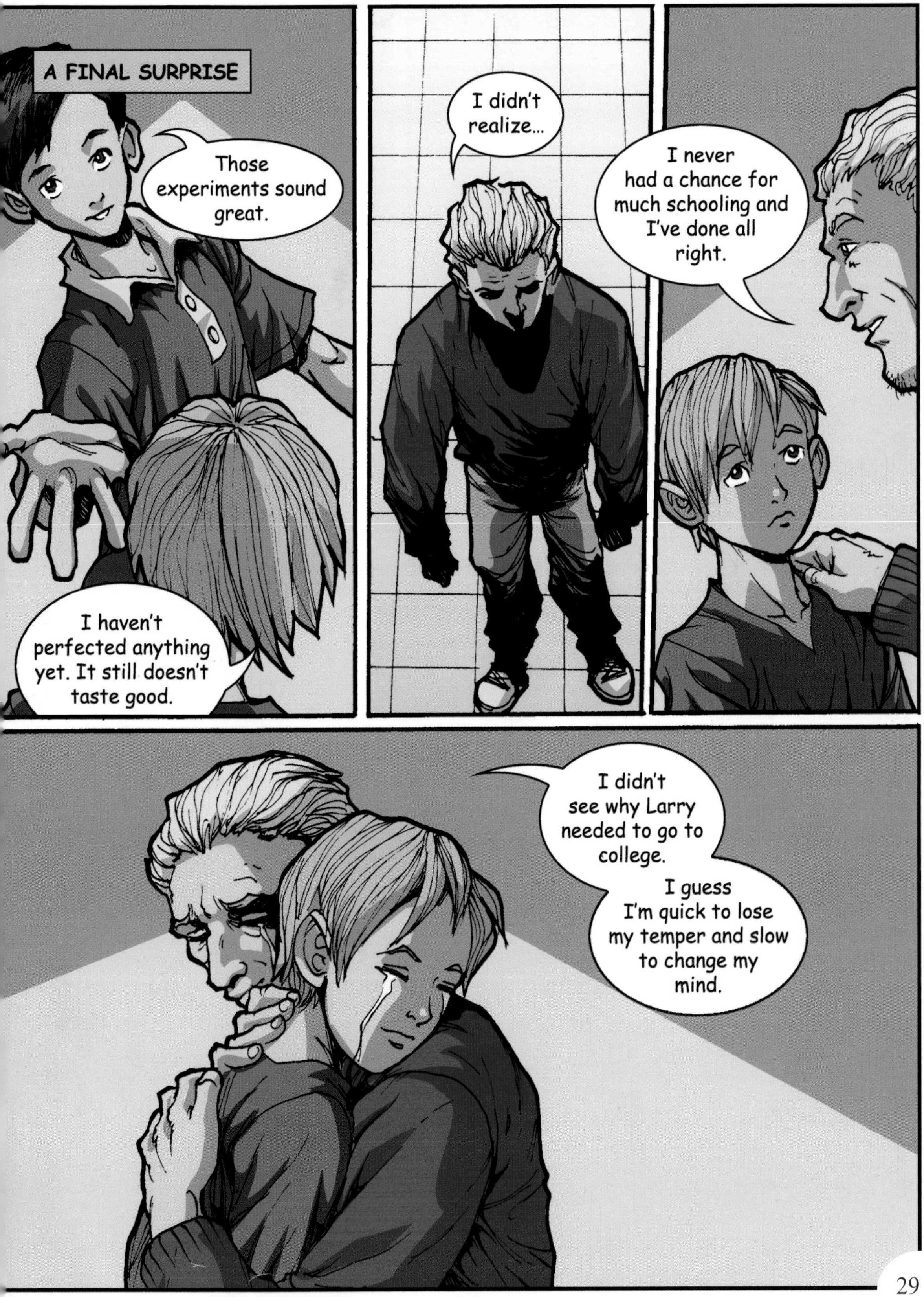
A FINAL SURPRISE
Those experiments sound great.
I haven't perfected anything yet. It still doesn't taste good.
I didn't realize...
I never had a chance for much schooling and I've done all right.
I didn't see why Larry needed to go to college.
I guess I'm quick to lose my temper and slow to change my mind.

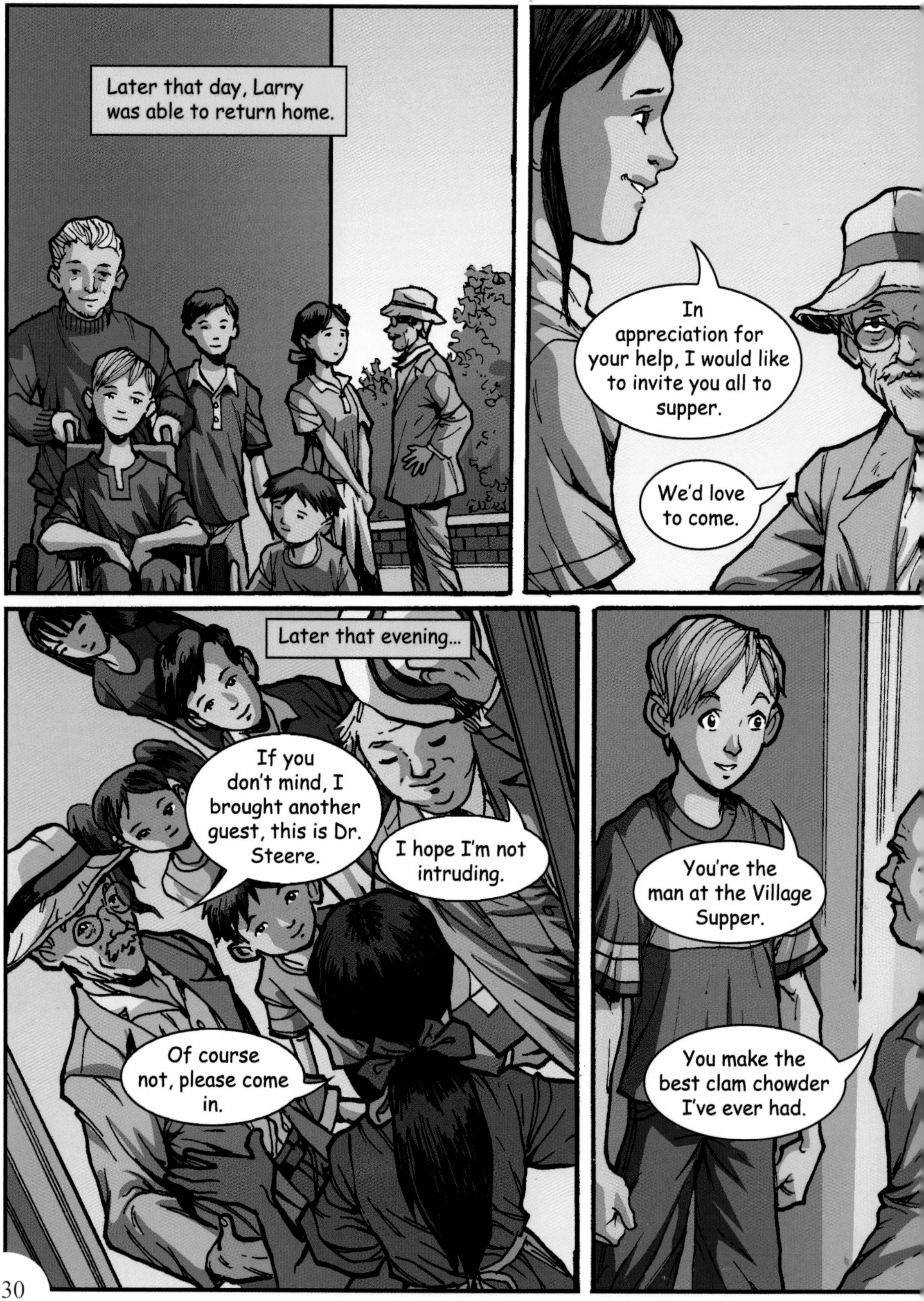
Later that day, Larry was able to return home.
In appreciation for your help, I would like to invite you all to supper.
We'd love to come.
Later that evening...
If you don't mind, I brought another guest, this is Dr. Steere.
I hope I'm not intruding.
Of course not, please come in.
You're the man at the Village Supper.
You make the best clam chowder I've ever had.

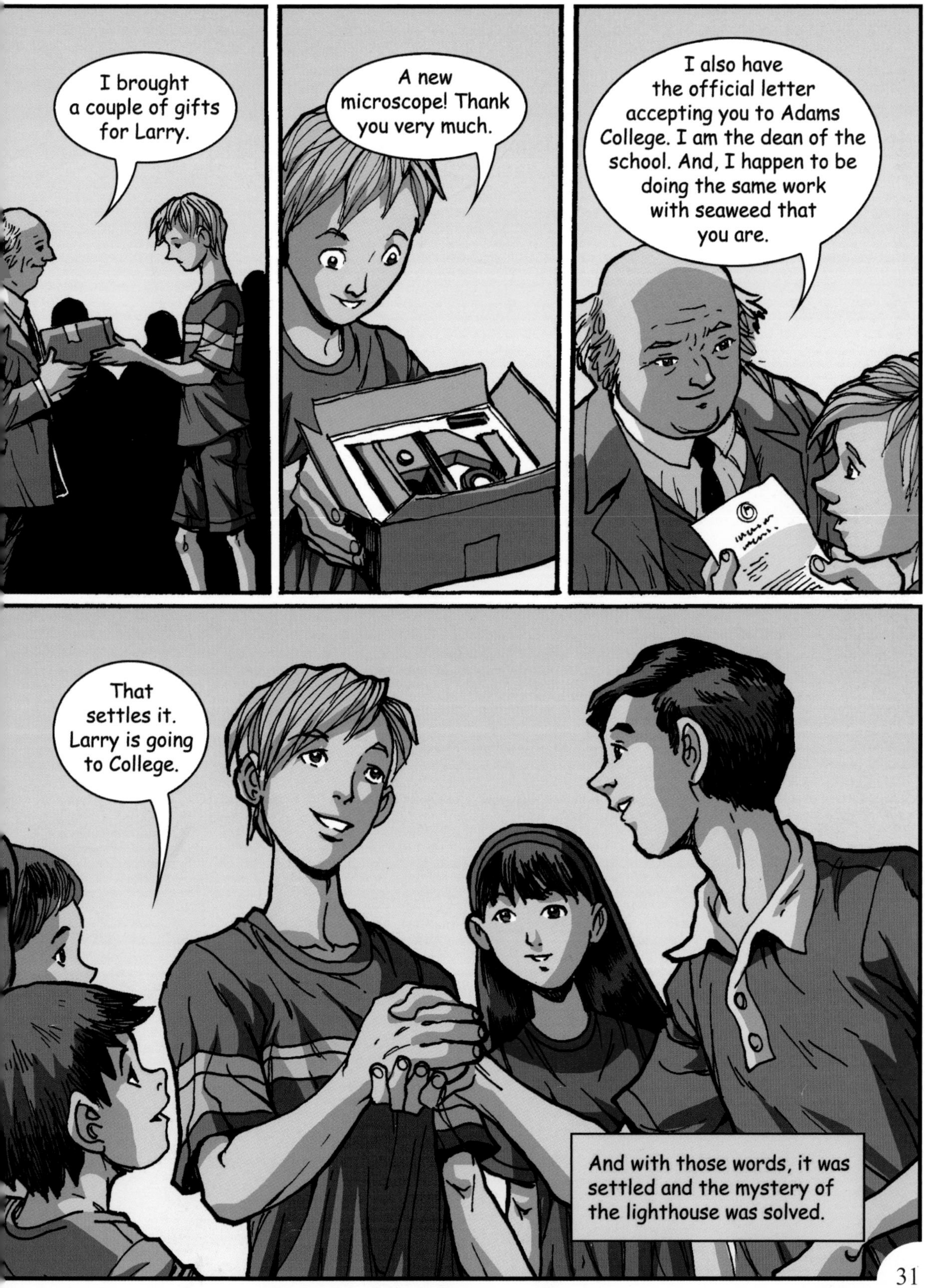
I brought a couple of gifts for Larry.
A new microscope! Thank you very much.
I also have the official letter accepting you to Adams College. I am the dean of the school. And, I happen to be doing the same work with seaweed that you are.
That settles it. Larry is going to College.
And with those words, it was settled and the mystery of the lighthouse was solved.

ABOUT THE CREATOR

Gertrude Chandler Warner was born on April 16, 1890, in Putnam, Connecticut. In 1918, Warner began teaching at Israel Putnam School. As a teacher, she discovered that many readers who liked an exciting story could not find books that were both easy and fun to read. She decided to try to meet this need. In 1942, *The Boxcar Children* was published for these readers.

Warner drew on her own experience to write *The Boxcar Children.* As a child she spent hours watching trains go by on the tracks near her family home. She often dreamed about what it would be like to live in a caboose or freight car—just as the Alden children do.

When readers asked for more Alden adventures, Warner began additional stories. While the mystery element is central to each of the books, she never thought of them as strictly juvenile mysteries. She liked to stress the Aldens' independence. Henry, Jessie, Violet, and Benny go about most of their adventures with as little adult supervision as possible—something that delights young readers.

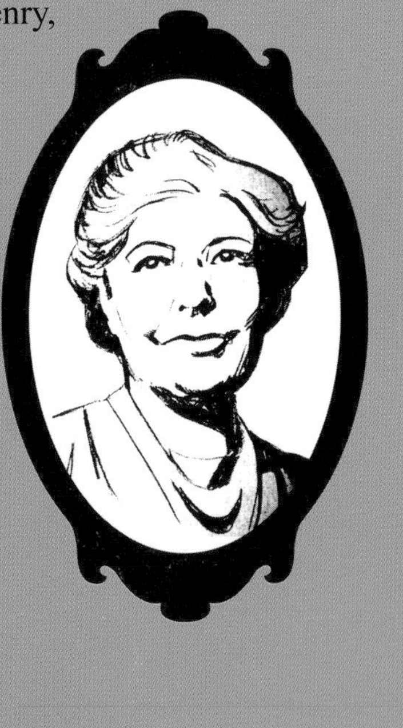

During her lifetime, Warner received hundreds of letters from fans as she continued the Aldens' adventures, writing nineteen Boxcar Children books in all. After her death in 1979, her publisher, Albert Whitman and Company, carried on Warner's vision. Today, the Boxcar Children series has more than 100 books.